BEWARE THE
Bantam Fighter

Stories

BEWARE THE Bantam Fighter

Stories

DAVID I. SANTIAGO

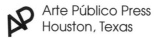
Arte Público Press
Houston, Texas

Beware the Bantam Fighter is funded in part through grants from the National Endowment for the Arts and the Texas Commission on the Arts. We are grateful for their support.

Recovering the past, creating the future

Arte Público Press
University of Houston
4902 Gulf Fwy, Bldg 19, Rm 100
Houston, Texas 77204-2004

Cover art by Jordanna Santiago
Cover design by Mora Des!gn

For my family

CONTENTS

BEWARE THE BANTAM FIGHTER

Josephina Burgos, with bags under her eyes, infant in hand and bawling child in lap, is a member of the parish council and a woman of purpose. She calms her sons on the steps of a three-flat they share with the López family, rubbing their backs, squeezing their hands, wiping their tears while her husband toils away at a box spring factory. In the house, her daughter sleeps, convalescing from chickenpox, while the pressure cooker hisses and the grandfather clock ticks.

"Who did this?" she asks again, inspecting the red bruise around her son's right eye.

The sobbing spasms continue but are less pronounced now, and the boy can finally point in the direction of the street corner. Josephina narrows her eyes, looking past the crumbling red brick facade next door, past the pothole pockmarks, past the sneakers hanging by their laces from the power lines, and focuses on the stop sign in the distance.

Soon, she has the youngest children in a red-striped tandem stroller on the sidewalk in front of the house, with her first son aching by her side. There is no hesitation, no doubt about her intentions. She is a mother hen, a Bantam

1

fighter walking into the pitter's entrance, ready to put on a show.

Señora Gonzales takes notice from the nearby bodega. The word spreads, and a crowd forms. "Something's happening," they say. "No one just walks like that."

There's a tug at Josephina's arm. "What's happening?" someone asks.

She struts down the street, head and chest held high, righteous indignation coursing through her veins. Who can match her intensity? Who can match her resolve?

Even the Spanish Cobras give her space, moving aside as she pushes the stroller past their turf, spectators behind her.

She feels her son's hand in her hand, gripping tightly now as they approach the street corner. The sun is high. Dust swirls around the base of the stop sign.

Two boys, two or three years older and bigger than her battered son, sit on BMX bicycles. One of them has a cigarette in his hand. Josephina pulls up in front of them. Her flock is behind her, arranged in a half circle.

She bends down, places her hands on her son's shoulders and looks into his eyes. They are brown, edged with red, still full of anxiety. He nods. She stands upright and places one hand on her hip. With the other hand, she points her index finger at them. There is no escaping her spur. Her words are like claws, filled with fury and truth.

They back away, shrinking and cowering. They clumsily place their feet on their pedals. Their bicycles wobble as they turn to leave. They collide with each other, crashing to the ground, pecked by her anger and bruised by concrete retribution.

They can't escape the shame. They can't defend themselves.

They are *caudillos* no more. This street corner, where they used fists and elbows to get their way, where they taunted and stole, where they smoked and drank, is dissolving into a derby pit where the score is already settled, and all they can do is pull themselves up and run.

THE CURSE

"Roberto, not again," said Josephina Burgos, groaning. "How many times must you tell that story?"

"But we love that story, Papi!" cried Ofelia. "Please tell it again, just this one time!"

Roberto took a sip of instant coffee from his mug and stared thoughtfully at his family, who had gathered around their white laminate-top dining room table. It was a cool, clear night in Chicago in 1978, and the neighborhood kids had gone home hours ago after filling their bags with Halloween treats.

Ofelia was sitting across the table from him, chewing on a Clark Bar, her eyes wide with anticipation. She was seven years old with short brown hair, big brown eyes and over-sized tortoise-shell glasses. Roberto's niece, Mercedes, was seated to Ofelia's right, next to her mother, Paola, who was his sister-in-law. Mercedes was six years old and had thick, raven-black hair like her mother. Roberto thought their Indio appearance was because of their Taíno blood, but it was impossible to know for sure.

Carlos, five years old, was sitting on Josephina's lap to Roberto's left, holding a cowboy hat he had worn earlier when trick-or-treating. Ten-year-old Luis was to Roberto's right. He was tall for his age and lanky, with black wavy hair like Roberto.

"I want to hear the story, too," said Carlos, looking up at Josephina imploringly.

"Yeah, let's hear it, Papi," said Luis.

Roberto smiled and turned toward Josephina.

"I guess I'm outnumbered!" Josephina huffed.

"*Mi querida*, Mercedes hasn't heard this story. And we are all here…"

"Tell us about the witch!" interjected Ofelia.

"Okay, okay," said Roberto, placing his hand on his wife's knee. "But I must get the blessing from *mi media naranja*. She is a critical part of this tale."

"Yes, fine, Roberto," said Josephina, chuckling. "Go ahead and tell the story. For Mercedes."

Roberto leaned into the table and shut his eyes. A hush fell over the room.

"I must have been around Luis' age," he began. "It was August 1961, and I was sitting on the front steps outside our home. It was a typical house on the outskirts of Fajardo, back in Puerto Rico, built of wood planks with a sheet metal roof. It was in a densely packed area, a squatter's community and most of our neighbors fished or worked cutting cane for the sugar mill.

"My mother was pregnant with my sister, your aunt Cassandra, and was about to go into labor. She was in the bedroom with my father and was tired and uncomfortable.

"My father had called for a midwife, and we—and by that, I mean my parents, me and two younger sisters—were all waiting for her to arrive. The air was thick and sticky in the house, and I had stepped outside to escape the oppressive heat, but it wasn't much better.

6

"My mother was sicker than usual with this pregnancy. Her ankles were badly swollen, and she had shortness of breath. We were all ready for the pregnancy to be over.

"I tossed a stick toward our small, tan mongrel, Duro, who was sitting under the shade of a banana tree. The dog stared momentarily at the stick, then shut its eyes. It was too hot to play. I sighed and tapped my bare feet on the rotting steps. I wanted to be away from there. I wanted to be in the water, exploring the mangroves for snapper or floating on my back in the lagoon. I thought of my father and how he could toss a fish net while standing on a wooden fishing boat in the rolling waves. He was born in Fajardo, a child of the water, and I wanted nothing more than to follow in his footsteps.

"A short while passed, and I saw an elderly black woman walking toward our house. She wore a white turban and an ankle-length white dress partially covered with a plain yellow apron. She trudged down the dirt road barefoot, holding a hand-woven basket filled with dried plants.

"I had never seen her before and thought she might have come over from the Dominican Republic or Haiti with one of the recent immigrant families. As she approached the house, Duro suddenly became aware of her presence and began barking. It paced nervously back and forth the closer she came, yapping incessantly until my father burst from the door of our house and tossed a rock at it.

"'I called for Doña Teresa,' said my father gruffly. He was a tall, proud man with skin as dark as the woman's, weathered from sun and salt. I could see he was tired and on edge, a sign to stand clear of him or else risk a lashing.

"'I am here for your wife,' said the woman calmly.

"My father glared at the woman, his arms crossed, and shook his head from side to side. 'No, I called for Doña Teresa. She delivered all our children.'

"In the distance, I heard the faint sound of thunder. Gray clouds were forming overhead.

"'Your wife is in trouble,' said the woman, standing a few feet away from the banana tree. 'Doña Tere sent me.'

"My sister Analilia poked her head out the front door and stared at the woman. She was nine years old and often helped my mother around the house.

"'Get back inside,' snapped my father.

"Analilia glanced at me, then retreated indoors.

"'What do you mean? How do you know she's is in trouble?' my father asked.

"There was another distant rumble, and I saw a small green lizard dart past my feet and under the stairs.

"'You must purify this house,' she said. 'I will help you. Then we can deliver the baby.'

"'This is no time for superstitious old women,' said my father. 'I will fetch Doña Teresa myself.'

"'There is no one to fetch. Doña Tere is dead.'

"My father placed his hand on his forehead. He was sweating, and his gray, short-sleeve shirt was soaked through. 'When did this happen?' he asked in a hushed voice.

"'Doña Tere died this morning at her home,' the old woman said, crossing her heart. 'I was with her, praying the Rosary.'

"My father said nothing for a minute or two as he stared at the darkening sky. There was a flash of light, and the wind picked up. 'I have never seen you before,' my father said eventually.

"'I live outside Fajardo. I came to see Doña Tere last week,' she said. 'I had a premonition about today.'

"My father seemed to have recovered his bad temper and suspicion. 'We are a God-fearing family,' he said. 'What are you?'

"'I am here to help you deliver your daughter,' she said. 'Doña Tere sent me.'

"My father scowled and came down the steps to approach the woman. 'I don't know why you think you can come here. Be gone, woman! We have nothing to do with witchcraft,' he said. He then turned to me and said, 'Roberto, go fetch Doña Gertrudis.'

"The woman faced me. I noticed her dark eyes were cloudy like the gathering storm. I was terrified. *How does she know my parents are having a daughter*? I thought.

"'The troubles are just beginning for you,' she said. 'Your family tree is branching and will splinter off in directions you cannot fully understand.'

"'Enough!' shouted my father, his fists balled together, ready to strike.

"'Yes, I have tried enough,' she said, turning to leave. 'The evil energies are traveling. God willing, they will not linger in your home, but I fear I am too late.'"

"Papi," interrupted Carlos. "Why didn't *abuelo* listen to the old lady?"

"Shh," said Luis.

"Let him finish the story, Carlos," said Ofelia.

Roberto twisted the end of his thick, black mustache and stared out the window. He could make out the hazy orange glow of the streetlamp from his seat.

"My father was quick to anger. His *pensamientos*, his thoughts, were angry that day. From stress and distrust of people different from himself. He never trusted Dominicans or Haitians. I cannot say why. And what you say in anger can become a *maldición*, a curse. What my father had not realized that day was that he had placed a curse on his family.

"Soon after my mother gave birth, the nature of the curse became apparent. Although the labor was thankfully free of complications, something was wrong with the newborn, Cassandra. She was born with gray clouds in her eyes, like the *bruja*. At first, we thought they might clear up, but after a month or so, it became obvious that she was not fully aware of the world around her. She had unusually fast eye movements and was restless and irritable. *Perhaps she is like my father,* I thought. *He never seems to stay still and has a quick temper.* And I was right. The evil energy the woman spoke of may have flown into Cassandra. But there was also, we soon discovered, the issue of cataracts.

"Congenital cataracts are very rare in children, but they afflict some people. And my poor baby sister was one of them. Unfortunately, we were also destitute and my parents did not get Cassandra the proper treatment in time to save her eyes, which is why she went blind. Had they sought help months earlier, Cassandra's outcome would have been better. But Cassandra's descent into blindness is a different, sad tale. We knew something was wrong with her, and that the *bruja's* prophecy had been correct.

"The full nature of her prophecy, however, had yet to be revealed. That happened a few weeks later, in late August," said Roberto.

"I was with my father early one Saturday morning on a secluded beach just north of the city, preparing to set lobster traps. The sun had not risen, and it was dark. My father and I would come to this beach often, where he had tied his *yola* to the base of a palm tree. He had built this boat by hand. It was painted navy blue and could fit about four people in its hull. He named it *Doncella*, his maiden. Rowing the *yola* in the sea was like a courtship dance, and he never took for granted that no matter how much he might try to coerce his *Doncella*, it was a fickle thing, readily influenced by the emotions of the water.

"This was storm season, and there were signs that the weather was turning. My father wanted to bring in one last catch before it was too dangerous to do so, and he also wanted to move his *yola* farther inland in case of a storm surge.

"I was baiting the wooden traps. This consisted of placing sardines in a mesh bag and then tying it to the trap's compartment near the entrance. The farther the lobsters moved into the trap's compartments, the more difficult it was for them to escape. We kept bricks in the *yola* and used them to help the traps sink upright on the ocean floor.

"After about an hour, we were ready to set off. We had finished preparing all the traps and had eaten a breakfast of chicken-filled *pastelillos*. My father always ate before he fished because he never knew how long he might be out on the water.

"The *yola* was not equipped with a motor, so muscles propelled the craft. My father was a vigorous man and had rowed for years in many conditions on the ocean. The oars were secured by mounted oarlocks on the gunwales. He sat on a bench in the center and pulled on the oars in a backward rowing position. I sat on a bench near the stern, sandwiched in between the lobster traps. It was dawning as we headed out toward the reef, but it was darker than normal and overcast. The ocean appeared relatively flat, with few whitecaps. It seemed to be a good day to fish.

"My father's demeanor quickly changed, however, as we rowed beyond the protection of the shore. There was a strong offshore wind, and my father had trouble maintaining a smooth rowing stroke. I could feel the ocean's pull, and the waves were getting choppier. That is the issue with the ocean. In a split second, before you've barely even ventured out on the water, it can suck you in and consume you. To those who say that our planet is Mother Earth, they are missing the obvious. Our planet mainly consists of great oceans that control and stabilize life, and people are completely at its mercy.

"'Roberto!' Father shouted above the grinding waves. 'Tie yourself down. Do it now!'

"I stared at my father. Panic gripped me when I saw the strain on his face as he tried to row the *yola* into the enlarging waves. There were whitecaps now, swelling in every direction, and the spray was beginning to affect visibility. We crested a rogue wave that was easily twice the height of the others, and I felt the boat accelerate as it descended, rolling the *yola* ominously to one side. The lobster traps slammed against the hull, and I would have been tossed into the open waters had I not been holding onto my seat.

"I tried to regain my composure. I pushed the traps at my feet toward the stern and got down with them, placing my legs under the bench so I was facing my father. I grasped the nautical rope connected to the traps and tried to find a loose end to tie myself down.

"'Cut the rope!' said my father, quickly reaching for the straight-blade knife attached to the belt on his pants and tossing it at my feet. 'Cut the rope for you and me!'

"My hands were shaking as I picked up the knife. I pulled a length of rope made of thick, entwined coir, and the blade did not easily slice through it. I heard *Doncella* groan and prayed that the blessed mother María was watching over us.

"'I can't turn back!' exclaimed my father. 'The winds are too strong!'

"I finally cut two pieces of rope, about five or six feet long. I tied one piece around my ankle and to my bench, then crawled over to my father and tied his ankle to his bench. At that point, with the spray and the powerful swells, we had no sighting of land. We were being pushed farther and farther out to sea. The wind was unrelenting.

"The expression about bad luck came momentarily to mind: *se vuelve sal y agua*, everything one touches turns to salt and water. Here we were, ruining our trawl lines, sitting in a tiny dinghy in a vast expanse of salt water. The *bruja's* premonitions were coming true. We were being carried away by evil energies.

"It began to rain. At first, it was a drizzle. Combined with the ocean spray, I took little notice. My heart was racing, and each swell brought the weight of the traps and bricks cascading painfully into my back. After about ten minutes, the rain intensified, and water came at us from all directions. My father appeared to be laboring; his tank top was soaked through, and the veins of his biceps were visibly bulging from exertion.

"'Roberto,' he said, gasping. 'Toss the bricks out!'

"I saw, to my horror, that the *yola* was filling with water quickly. The water and our gear were weighing the *yola* down, causing my father to strain with the extra burden. I grabbed the bricks and threw them overboard, one at a time, while always keeping one hand firmly grasped on the bench or gunwales.

"'The bucket!' shouted my father, pointing to a small bait bucket floating between us. 'Bail the water!'

"For the next hour, the storm battered the *Doncella*. There was an explosion of water and thunder and lightning. I prayed and prayed and bailed and bailed. My father toiled with the oars, his strokes becoming shorter to keep the *yola* centered. We rode the waves up and down, each wave was like a formless opponent we had to vanquish. My stomach churned as we were pushed farther out into the ocean, and I could not envision us doing this for much longer. And just when it seemed like we were at our breaking point, as suddenly as the wind, the rain and the waves had appeared, the storm subsided, and all was calm.

"We must have been on the water for an hour and a half at that point, but it seemed like days. The sky cleared, and the *yola* rolled gently up and down in the waves. The *Doncella* was still heavy with water, but my father and I were too exhausted to care. We could feel the morning sun on our backs, and we both shut our eyes and lowered our heads over our chests while we idly floated in the empty waters.

"I woke a short while later to the lapping of waves against the *Doncella*. The sun was rising overhead, and the air was still. My father was bailing water from the hull of the *yola*. This was a tedious process with such a small bucket, and I tried to help by scooping water out with my hands. Another hour passed, and the *Doncella* was mostly free of water, except for puddles around our feet. My father was lightly rowing to keep the boat stable but did not appear to have a destination in mind. His eyes were fixed blankly on the horizon. We said nothing, and I knew we were lost.

"By midday, the sun was hot overhead, and my lips were chapping. The saliva in my throat felt like sandpaper, and I felt weak. My father stared at me, and I saw tears in his eyes. The constant anger and the frequent eruptions that characterized him had dissolved, and there was a tenderness I had not seen before. 'I should have listened to the *bruja*,' he said at last. 'Turn around. Let me see your back.'

"I rose unsteadily in the *yola* and turned toward the stern, with my back facing my father. 'You lost blood,' he said, examining my back.

"I felt his hands lifting up my white tank top. He pressed a wet cloth into my lumbar region. 'Hold this, *nene*. You'll be fine.'

"I held the cloth against my back and turned to face him. He had taken off his shirt and was bare-chested in the sun. 'Are we far from land?' I asked.

"'No, we can't be,' he said. 'Tonight, if we can't find our way back, we will use the stars to guide us.'

"I fell into an uneasy sleep. I was lying on the water-logged bottom boards, with my head resting against the curve of the yola's frame, sandwiched next to the lobster traps, which smelled of sardines and saltwater. I had my arm over my eyes to shield me from the sun, but I could still see bright yellow and orange stars under my eyelids. I came in and out of consciousness, waking abruptly when the yola rolled heavily to one side, or my father shifted his weight to stretch his weary arms and legs.

"'Stand up,' said a voice in my head.

"'I cannot,' I responded in my thoughts. 'I will sleep the sleep of death.'

"'You will stand up. Now!' commanded the voice.

"I rose and found myself not in the Doncella but standing on a tranquil turquoise sea. From the depths of the waters, I saw a dark woman rising, wearing a sargassum turban and dress, surrounded by a glistening school of whirling sardines. 'Where am I?' I asked in my dream.

"The woman stood over the waters and stared at me through her deep, blue-black eyes. 'You are in the tears of your father,' she said.

"'What am I doing here?' I asked, shuddering.

"'You are here to cleanse yourself of his troubled spirit,' she said.

"The woman stepped forward and reached out her hand. 'Come to me.'

15

"I walked over to her, and she grasped my right hand. I felt an electric shock course through my veins. There was no pain, just a current of warmth.

"'I will immerse you in your father's tears to clear the balance,' she said, gently spinning me around and leaning me backward until my face was momentarily beneath the waters. All around me, I could see millions of sardines circling as if warding off any predators trying to harm me. I opened my mouth in awe, and as the water rushed in, I could taste rum and salt.

"I felt pressure on my back as the woman lifted me up out of the waters. When I surfaced, I was back on the *Doncella,* sitting upright and fully awake. My father had been staring at me, and he smiled as I rubbed my head.

"'Welcome to the world of the living, my son,' he said. 'We will be home soon. Although I cannot see it, I can feel it in my bones.'

"We had been on the water for nearly twelve hours when we heard a sound that startled us. At first, I thought it was my imagination, but as my father continued to row, the sound became more distinct, resembling the staccato of a drum. 'Look, over there!' he shouted, pointing over his shoulder. Even though I was facing the bow of the *yola,* I was exhausted and had not noticed the contours of the shoreline in the distance or the large vessel approaching us. It was difficult to make out the ship at first, and my father rowed with renewed energy to make sure we intercepted it. Another thirty minutes passed, and this time, the ship was coming into full view. It was a large, steel-plated naval landing ship riding high, displacing great swaths of water as it raced toward us.

"My father picked up his bloodied tank top from the *yola's* hull and gingerly stood on his seat, waving the shirt and shouting, 'Help us!¡*Ayúdennos!*'

"I joined my father, stood up and began waving my hands. I could make out the white hull number, 1176, below the 50-caliber mounted guns.

"A metal rescue craft was deployed from the ship, not much larger than our *Doncella*. Four US Naval officers were in the boat, and one was carrying a fifteen-foot hook. 'Hey, there!' said a sailor, standing on the craft's stern with a white-and orange-striped lifebuoy in one hand. 'This is a United States Navy live impact area. It's off limits!'

"Another sailor joined him at the stern and stared at us.

"'You look like you're in bad shape. Do you need a lift?'

"'Yes. Please help,' said my father. 'We come from Fajardo.'

"'Fajardo? What the heck are you doing out here in a rowboat?'

"'*El viento nos llevó.*'

"'What did he say?' asked the man with the lifebuoy.

"'He said the wind blew them out here,' said the other sailor as he extended the boathook to our *yola*. 'Jesus, let's get you towed back to base. You're at the Vieques Naval Training Range.'

"A direct route from Fajardo to Vieques Island by motorized boat would usually take ninety minutes. Many vessels were traveling back and forth between the islands daily. But our *yola* was blown off course and spun around the currents near Culebra before drifting south toward the eastern part of Vieques. My father said that we were saved by the grace of God, and had we missed the island, we could have ended up in the middle of the Atlantic headed toward Africa.

"The sailors towed us to port, and from there, they helped us make arrangements with a commercial fisherman sailing to Fajardo that evening. He was an elderly man with a gray beard and bleached, long-brim Panama hat. He met us at the naval base in his thirty-foot, diesel-powered fishing vessel, with the word *Greenpoint* painted on the side of the hull. 'Follow me,' he said, directing us inside his boat, where he handed my father a tow line and pointed to the bow eye. 'Tie it down here and then to the stern of your boat. You can ride with me if you want.'

"My father made a bowline knot and leaped out of the boat into the shallow waters, wading a short distance to the *Doncella* to secure it. I watched my father handle the line with ease, letting it slide through his hands as he allotted enough space for the *yola* to be towed at a safe distance from the fishing vessel. He was comfortable in the water. It was what he knew.

"I leaned my back against the gunwales of the *Greenpoint* and stared at the sky. The sun was setting, and the sky was blue, pink and cloudless. *I will not be getting back into the yola*, I thought."

"Is that why you left Puerto Rico?" interjected Mercedes. "You didn't really want to be like your father, after all?"

Roberto smiled and took a sip of his coffee, which was now cold. He stood up, stepped back from his chair, placed his hands behind his back and looked at the clock on the wall.

"It is said that the spirits of *brujas* allow them to see into the future," Roberto said, still looking at the clock. "My father's anger, his problems with drinking, I should add, were not uncommon sins. But when directed at a *bruja*, the evil energies rebounded and were passed on to subsequent generations. To Cassandra. To myself."

"Are they passed on to us?" asked Mercedes.

"What I can say is that seven years after my father and I were swept to Vieques, when I was old enough to leave Fajardo, I left for Brooklyn. For a neighborhood called Greenpoint. The US mainland was where I wanted to be."

"What your father, your uncle, is trying to say is that he was cursed into marrying me!" said Josephina, laughing.

Roberto turned around, frowning. "*Mi querida*, stop teasing. It was no curse meeting you in Greenpoint. It was a *bendición!*"

"I think when I am older," said Ofelia, "I would like to become a *bruja*. One that helps people."

"Very well. And if you become a *bruja*, just remember that you don't ride broomsticks and wear pointy hats on Halloween," said Roberto. "You will have a clean and beautiful spiritual power to help others understand the causes of their troubles. 'There is no coincidence, just causality,' so the expression goes. Or at least, that is what I saw. And that is what I felt, in the depths of my bones, on the water that day."

WHEN WE WANDER

It is a gray, musty day in 1973. We are traveling from San Juan to Guaynabo in a red Datsun 510. The car is dented and rusting around the sills and floor pans. My father is trying to calm my mother on the passenger seat. Sweat trickles down the back of his neck, and his black hair is damp and curling from the humidity. My mother sits with arms crossed over her swollen belly and is staring out the window.

"You're lost," she huffs as we drive down the street for the third time in thirty minutes.

My father flips through a Rand McNally atlas of Puerto Rico and settles on an intricately detailed page of the San Juan area. He traces his finger along a line on the map.

"It's been a while," he mumbles.

A car horn blares, and my father swerves back into his lane.

"*¡Ay, Dios!*" my mother cries. Then, turning to me, she says, "Luis, tighten your seatbelt!"

We finally make it up the mountain. My sister, Ofelia, is two years old and fast asleep, while I'm three years her senior and trying to stay awake. Everything is different here. It had been snowing at home in Chicago when we left for Puerto Rico the day after Christmas. My father had managed to get us discounted tickets, but we had to leave before dawn, and everyone was tired.

We turn into a narrow gravel road and pull up to a white, concrete block house surrounded by palm and banana trees. A chalky chihuahua slips through the iron bars on the porch and runs up to our car, yapping at us like we are intruders.

"That's Blackie," says my dad.

Ofelia rubs her eyes and peers out the window. A woman steps out of the house, wiping her hands against her apron. She looks just like my mother. She has shoulder-length, light brown hair and a broad smile.

"*Bendición*, Mamá," says my father as he steps out of the car next to the barking dog.

"*Dios te bendiga.*"

The next day, I am with my cousin Jason. He is eleven and doesn't talk much, but we get along just fine. We are taking a shortcut down a hill through an overgrown dirt path to another cousin's house. Jason is swinging a machete to clear away ferns and low-lying shrubs. As a Boy Scout, he knows how to navigate the forests around our families' properties. Two years ago, he showed me how to tie a fisherman's knot, but I can't remember how to do it anymore.

We come to a two-story house on the edge of a cliff; it is held up by stilts on the downslope side so that it rises high above the forest canopy below. The ground around the house is wet, and my gym shoes are caked in mud as we approach. He has something to show me.

Under the house's foundation, there are all sorts of things: bicycles, pieces of wire fencing, plywood, old car tires. A weathered, tannish mutt stares at us through one open eye from on top of a cardboard box as he battles sleep.

Jason points his machete at a three-foot-by-three-foot cage between two car tires. Inside the cage, a black-breasted red bantam swivels its head toward us. Its red comb and wattles have been removed, making it look like an angry pheasant.

The bantam seems to get more agitated as we approach, bobbing its head as it struts back and forth in the cage. It reminds me of a Bengal tiger I saw once at the Lincoln Park Zoo that paced in its cell, its large head weaving from side to side, probably dreaming of its native home in the jungle.

Jason and I crouch down beside the cage to get a closer look. The bantam backs away but continues to strut and puff out its feathers. A hooked-shaped, razor-sharp steel blade is attached to its right leg. It doesn't look comfortable, and the bantam glares at us as it moves about the cage.

"He's a champion," says Jason, flexing his biceps and then jabbing the air a couple of times.

Jason stands up and beckons me up around the back entrance to the house. "Come." He has more to show me.

I try to stand up but can't take my eyes off the rooster. It looks miserable, angry and proud, all wrapped in one. Its long, black tail feathers give it a regal air.

I hear Jason calling me again, and as I stand to leave, I notice a rusted padlock on the front door of the cage. Its lock hasp is in the staple, but it isn't secured. I glance over my shoulder to see if Jason is in view, and seeing that he isn't, I slowly open the cage's gate.

On the last day of our trip to Puerto Rico, Ofelia and I are lying on our stomachs on the porch's concrete floor next to Abuelo, drawing with chalk. Abuelo is dozing off on a rocking chair to the sound of a *telenovela* playing inside.

A little while later, Abuela comes out, bringing us orange juice. She kneels beside us to examine our artwork.

Ofelia has drawn misshapen hearts of varied sizes and colors. She has chalk dust all the way up to her elbows.

"It is good to share your heart," says Abuela.

Ofelia beams while sucking orange juice through a straw.

My drawings are a little less abstract. My favorite is the yellow iguana.

Abuela glances at the drawing of the blue-and-red bantam next to Abuelo's feet. "Daniel Narváez came over last night looking for his prizefighter. He said it was lost," she says.

My eyes are fixed on the floor.

"I offered him my condolences. I hoped to see him at church." She places her hand on my shoulder and continues. "These men, what they do is no good. Birds are meant to wander. Nothing is lost."

❧∽❧∽❧

I am ten years old. We pull up to Abuela's house, and a brown chihuahua slips through the iron bars on the porch and runs up to our car, ferociously yapping at us.

"That's Blackie," says Dad.

Abuela steps out of the house, her hair now dyed auburn.

"*Bendición,* Mamá," says my father as he steps out of the car next to the barking dog.

"*Dios te bendiga.*"

We are all sitting around the dining room table for supper. We are having *arroz con habichuelas* and *pollo guisado*. This is the first proper meal on the island for my little brother, Carlos. I can smell the *recao*. It is the smell of Puerto Rico.

Abuelo is sitting in between Abuela and me, barely eating. He wears a blank expression.

A *telenovela* is playing softly in the background. Abuela explains that on this soap opera episode, Antonio is told that he has amnesia and must return to his wife, whom he doesn't remember.

Mom explains that amnesia is when you lose your memory. I wonder what that is like; especially what it's like to not recognize your wife or your family. Without memory, who are we? All the moments and feelings are gone.

"Our memories are the ingredients of this dinner," says Abuela. "They become part of us, sustaining us, even if later we don't remember having them."

The next afternoon, I was coming back from Tía Cusie's house with Jason. It had just rained, one of those heavy downpours that last not much longer than a game of HORSE. We took turns shooting a basketball into the net. I'd always lose against Jason, spelling horse with each missed shot. We were soaked, having decided not to stop the game during the rain shower, but the sun was out, and we were fine.

Jason dribbles the basketball around puddles as we walk up the road to Abuelo and Abuela's house. At the turn just beyond Julio's pork stand, a *lechonera*, we hear a great rustling in the woods. Jason approaches a thicket of bamboo and reaches in. He pulls out a man by his wrist.

Covered in grime and wet, the man stumbles to the side of the road. His feet are bare, his tank top and pants are torn, and he has a 9th Infantry Division baseball cap on his head. He is holding a bottle in a wet paper bag and is nodding affirmatively.

"They are here."

Jason, still gently holding the man's wrist, looks into his bloodshot eyes. They are the eyes of a man with a type of pain that clouds his vision.

"It's over, Don José. It's over."

I am eleven and sitting on our living room couch. On the floor beside me is Indigo, our next-door neighbor's German Shepherd, who we watch when they are away. My dad calls him Blackie.

The phone rings and I hear my dad's voice.

"*Bendición*, Mamá."

"*Dios te bendiga.*"

My mother steps away from the kitchen and joins my father. I think of Guaynabo, the green hills, and the call of the roosters each morning. I can smell the *recao* and feel the dense, damp air on my skin.

It is June in Chicago, and the dandelions are out, poking their yellow flowers through the cracks in the sidewalk. I want to take a machete and chop my way through the weeds and grasses in the alley behind us. Maybe the bantam I freed is here, keeping the street clean of rats.

When my father comes out, he tells me about Jason, how he waded into the water after a Boy Scout who was drowning. They were attempting to ford the river, but the one scout wandered too deep and was pulled under. Jason tried to save him but was pulled in, too.

Jason is a memory now, and my eyes are burning. I cannot see or think and bury my head in the couch cushions. I have never cried in front of my parents like this. I am miserable, angry and proud, all wrapped in one. No, he is *not* lost. He is the champion, the bantam. He is a part of me.

I am sixteen years old, accompanying my aunt to Abuela's house. A gray Chihuahua slips through the iron bars on the porch and runs up to our car.

"That's Blackie," says Aunt Cusie.

Abuela steps out of the house, her hair now gray.

"Titi, why do I always see different dogs here?"

Tía Cusie pulls up the parking brake and stares at the dog. "There are many reasons. The last one wandered off and was hit by a car. The dogs here are always wandering."

Later that week, I am working for my aunt's new husband, Orlando. We are building a fence. I mix cement with sand, stone and water in a wheelbarrow. My face is red, and I am drenched in sweat. Orlando hands me a bottle of water, then scoops a shovelful of the cement mixture into the wooden fence post forms. He is strong and lean, never slowing down as he chats with the other workers.

I'm having a hard time following their conversation, but we get along fine. When the cement mixture runs low, I prepare new batches. Orlando and I are a team, and the money for the job is good.

That evening, I finished dinner with Tía Cusie and Orlando. I am tired and sore from the fence-building.

"I will take you back to Abuela's," says Tía Cusie.

"No, I can walk," I say. "I won't get lost."

Before I leave, I give Orlando a hat I bought with the money I earned from working with him. It is a camouflage-colored baseball hat that will keep the sun out of his eyes.

Orlando gives me a big smile and lightly punches my shoulder. We all hug, and I wander up the road back to Abuela's house.

It is night, and I hear the *coquís* chirping and a donkey braying. Blackie is snoring by my feet on the bed. There are many pictures on the wall of the guest bedroom. There is a picture of Abuelo next to a red fire station in Ponce. He is young, like me, but darker. His memories are our memories. Not the exact memories but contours of the memories passed from generation to generation. I can feel them all around me, even though he is not here anymore.

There is another picture of Tía Cusie and Jason. These memories are sharper. Jason is standing behind Tía Cusie, who is sitting on a chair. He is wearing his Boy Scout uniform and is about the same age as me. The photo must have been taken weeks before the accident.

Jason is a Boy Scout and never gets lost. He may have wandered, but he is still here, a part of me, a part of us. He is the Bengal tiger, now free to roam the jungles of India. He is the bantam, now free of his cage. He is Blackie, along with all the other Blackies, now free of the callousness of men. He is me, and I am as much Tía Cusie and Orlando's son as the son of my mother and father.

We are family, and our memories live on, even when we wander.

MY LITTLE *LUCHADOR*

This child is stubborn. I tell him, "Carlos, get up. You'll miss the bus." But *no*, he pulls the covers over his head and curls up in a ball.

"*Presta mucha atención a lo que estoy por decir,*" I warn. "Listen to what I'm going to say: Get up *now!*"

Carlos unfurls the covers and glares at me, forehead wrinkled, lips curled down. It is a quarter to seven, and the bus arrives in fifteen minutes. I will not walk him to school again.

"I don't want to go!" he cries.

I place my hands on my hips and stare out the window. The López boys are waiting at the bus stop, bundled in winter jackets, mittens, boots, caps with pom-poms and backpacks. They are stomping on snow and prepared to start the day.

"At least you're being honest with me today," I say.

"I didn't feel well yesterday!" he protests.

"Uh-huh."

I glance at my watch. This is a game of chicken. Who will step aside first?

Then I think about Ofelia and Luis. How his being late causes them to be late, which causes *me* to be late for work. *It just doesn't let up!*

"I'll buy you a Snickers," I say, caving, staring at the wall with pursed lips.

The room is quiet now, except for the radiator clicking. I hold my breath.

A minute later, still looking ahead, mustering as much dignity as possible, I hear the bed sheets ruffle. A floorboard creaks. The patter of steps. A drawer opening and slamming shut. The running of the faucet. More steps approach the room, abruptly halt, then retreat. A crash in the hallway. The sound of papers rustling and a zipper grinding shut. Steps retreat to the room. Heavy breathing.

I look down and see Carlos. His shoes are on the wrong feet. The zipper on his pants is undone, and his jacket is unbuttoned. His backpack isn't closed either and crumpled papers stick out.

"Very good," I say, zipping up his jeans and buttoning his jacket. Then I switch his shoes. "Let's..." I pause, staring at his cowlick. A tuft of black hair rises from his crown like a rooster's comb.

"Now, wait one second," I say, grabbing a brush from the nearby dresser. I brush it down, but it pops back up. "Come on," I say. "Down you go, you Devil's horn!"

It pops back up. I spit on my palm and rub it down, but it pops back up. I sit Carlos on the edge of the mattress, pushing and pulling, smoothing and ruffling his hair, until Carlos cries, "¡Mami! Stop!"

I sigh. It is five past seven, and the bus has come and gone. I place my hands on Carlos' chubby cheeks and kiss him on the forehead.

"My little *luchador*," I say. "Hold my hand. I will walk you to school."

THE SCALE OF THE OCEAN

Luis Burgos was standing next to his grandmother, Ignacia, in her backyard in Guaynabo, staring up at a towering coconut palm tree he was about to scale. They were to make *caldo santo* to celebrate the Lenten season and nothing but the finest, freshest ingredients would do.

"Your *abuelo* cut grooves into the trunk, like a ladder," said Ignacia. "He used to climb this tree barefoot, but you should wear your sneakers."

Luis looked at his feet. He had recently turned thirteen and had experienced a growth spurt. His feet had now reached size seven. He heard a door swing open and slam shut and turned to see his younger brother, Carlos, walking toward them.

"What's happening?" Carlos asked.

"I need to scale this tree," said Luis.

Carlos looked up at the tree and sucked in his breath. "That will be hard!"

"I can do it," said Luis with false bravado.

Luis studied the grayish-brown trunk and its ring scars from fallen palm fronds. He would use the ring scars and grooves to help him grip and push up from the trunk.

"And you think a straight tree like this one is easier to scale than a bent one, like the one over there, Abuela?" Luis asked, pointing to a neighboring coconut palm.

Ignacia handed Luis a large burlap bag. "Yes, it will be easier," she said. "But I can ask your cousin to scale it instead. I would never forgive myself if you fell."

Luis glanced at Carlos, who was gazing at him. "No, Abuela, it's okay," he said. "I will not fall."

Luis placed the bag's strap over his shoulder and walked to the base of the tree, rubbing his right hand over the scratchy bark. He was grateful that he was wearing jeans.

At home, in Humboldt Park, Luis and his neighborhood friends would often try to outdo each other during recess or after school, with each kid constantly vying for status as a top athlete. During baseball practice, they tried to hit the ball the farthest or steal the most bases. But there were other opportunities as well, such as scaling various objects in the form of parkour and performing aerial flips and jumps. Sometimes, this was done in the presence of girls, who they thought would be impressed. They would climb up telephone poles, fences, garbage bins and streetlamps, all in the most fluid and acrobatic manner possible. Luis was comfortable with heights and not afraid to accept a dare. He had developed some of his mother's fearlessness, and he assumed she had acquired her fearlessness from Abuela and Abuelo. But he was a little nervous now. He had never climbed something this tall before.

"Abuela, why do we need coconuts?" asked Carlos.

"We will add coconut milk to the soup we are making tonight," said Ignacia. "It will balance out the flavors, so our broth has both the sweetness from the coconut and the saltiness from the *bacalao*. So much of what we do in life is about balance."

"I'm ready," said Luis.

He took a step back and leaped onto the swollen base of the tree, hugging it tightly while securing his feet onto one of the bottom grooves. He brought his knees toward his chest and pushed his feet off a higher set of grooves, then lifted his arms over his head and repeated the hopping motion all over again. Soon, he was at the tree's crown and leaned his right elbow onto a thick frond midrib to help support his weight.

Luis looked to his side and could see the forested canopy of the valley below. He hadn't realized that his grandparents' house was on such a high mountain ridge. He could see pink and red dots mixed with the various shades of green, which he assumed were from the flowering Mara trees he had seen on the way up to his grandparents' property when they first arrived last weekend.

A warm gust of air shook the palm fronds, and he felt the tree sway and his adrenaline surge. He was on top of the world, with a bird's eye view of Guaynabo. He was a mapmaker, cataloging the contours of the land in his mind, documenting the position of the sun, and noting features in scale. Never had he scaled something so high, so majestic, so elemental to a heritage, to a place he was only starting to understand. He knew he would never forget the way he felt up there.

He turned his attention to the cluster of brown coconuts under the palm fronds. He reached out his left hand and grabbed the one closest to him, twisting it like Ignacia had instructed. Luis had to twist it several times before the fruit detached from the stem.

"I don't think I can keep my balance and put it in the bag," he shouted to Ignacia as he cradled the coconut between his forearm and bicep.

"Just drop it," replied Ignacia. "It will be fine."

Ignacia stood back from the tree, pulling Carlos by the shirt collar toward her. Luis scanned the ground below and dropped the coconut on a bed of soft grass.

"It's heavy!" said Carlos, picking up the coconut and shaking it.

"Can you hear the water inside?" asked Ignacia.

Carlos shook the coconut again, placing his ear close to it. "Yes, I can hear something!"

"Good, that means that the coconut is ready," said Ignacia.

A short while later, Ignacia and Luis were in the kitchen. On the countertop, Ignacia had arranged the coconuts, a large, whole red snapper, cod fish (which had been soaking for hours in water), manioc root, squash, green plantains, onions, garlic, olives, capers, bay leaves, *adobo*, annatto seeds, salt, pepper, vegetable stock and *sofrito*. She had already made a large pot of *arroz con gandules*.

"I really want to learn how to make this *caldo santo*," said Luis.

"It's not hard to do this soup," said Ignacia. "First, you will need to slice the onions and cut the *calabaza* and *yuca*."

Luis picked up one of the yellow onions and began slicing it, peeling away the parchment-like skin. "Why do you always cook it during this time of the year?"

"Because Lent is a time when we scale back," said Ignacia. "It is a period of grief, leading up to Easter."

"How fine should I chop these?" asked Luis.

"Just like you have done," said Ignacia. "You can cut the *calabaza* and *yuca* into small chunks when you are done with the onions."

34

Ignacia grabbed the snapper by the tail, placed it under the faucet and rinsed it to loosen the skin.

"Next, we will simmer the onions, *calabaza* and *yuca* in water. You can fill more than half the pot with water when you're ready. We need to make soup for our whole family."

Ignacia grabbed a knife and began scaling the snapper with the blunt end. "This is a special dish," she continued. "I always thought there was a richness in it because it was made through sacrifice. In our case, we're not eating meat." It represents our cultural richness..."

"There are many ingredients," said Luis.

"Yes, because a proper *caldo santo* is like a window of history," said Ignacia. "The water, that is the ocean, so vast in scale, which surrounds this island. We cook the soup at a simmer to avoid introducing a bad energy, offsetting the texture's balance, like a storm."

Ignacia placed the snapper on a cutting board and began gutting it.

"The *yuca*, the squash and the snapper belonged to the Taíno. It is said they migrated to Puerto Rico from the Amazon, but who knows for sure? The scale of time is unmeasurable. There is so much movement back and forth in the Caribbean.

"Some say the Taíno have disappeared.... But all you must do is look around. They are here, in this dish. They are part of us.

"There was a woman at church who used to say the *indios* were heathens and died because of God's judgment. 'Puerto Ricans are Spanish,' she said, even though she was blacker than most.

"I say, yes, some Puerto Ricans are Spanish, but most Puerto Ricans are what you see in this dish. We know the Spanish, our ancestors, placed their thumbs on the scale of justice as they attempted to take this land. But they could never do so as Spaniards because this land changed them. The Taíno, they stewed in this pot with the Spanish, their flavors merging, their colors changing, their ties deepening, their understanding of who they were and what they were thickening into a new reality.

"Then the slaves came. Brought from markets along the West African coast and who knows where else. They were forced to board cargo ships on boiling waters through the Middle Passage, to cut sugarcane in the island lowlands. Forced to ensure that the insatiable demand for sugar was met. They replaced the Taíno, who were fast disappearing.

"But under such circumstances, people resisted. They tipped the scale back to where it belongs. They were not just laborers; they were, we can assume, fishermen, gardeners, poets and merchants. They were people from all walks of life who blended with the Spanish and the Taíno. They introduced plantains and *gandules*. The coconut you just harvested was also from the Old World but brought here by the Spanish.

"In *caldo santo,* we celebrate the Trinity: the three origins of the ingredients that make us who we are today. Created in the image of God, we are perfect as we are. There is no need to elevate one ingredient over the other. Let's celebrate the balance that has been achieved and toss in other ingredients as our land transforms before our eyes, faster now and right under our feet. We will widen our pot as more ingredients arrive, as people come and go, and as we learn more about what it means to live off the island but to be *of* the island."

Ignacia placed her chef's knife on the cutting board and turned her attention toward Luis. Outside, the *coquíes* could be heard chirping.

"You look so much like your mother," she said finally. "I see it most of all in your eyes—those deep, amber eyes."

Luis returned her gaze and noticed the same amber color in *her* eyes, like the hackle feathers of the Bantam rooster he had seen in front of the house earlier in the day.

"For me, this day is a gift," said Ignacia. "My children have all left the island, but I know the island has not left them."

"It won't leave me either, Grandma," said Luis, walking over to her and placing his arm around her shoulders. "This day *is* a gift. Earlier, when I was at the top of the coconut tree, the ocean seemed smaller, the distance separating Chicago from Guaynabo was not so big. For me, that distance was nothing at all."

JUAN BOBO, THE GUARDIAN ANGEL

"What happened today must not happen again," said Roberto, leading eight-year-old Carlos up the steps of their three-story flat.

"Sit here." Roberto gestured toward a white plastic patio chair next to their front door.

He took off his broad-shoulder navy blue blazer and folded it neatly over the concrete porch slab nearest the gangway. It was early April but unusually warm. He had left work early for a physical. On the way home from the doctor's office that afternoon, he had witnessed the incident.

"You have a guardian angel, Carlos. I recognized the López boys. And Joel Ortiz. But there was another."

Carlos sulked in his chair.

"What was his name again?"

"Juan, Papi," said Carlos.

"Ah! Just as I thought… *Juan.*"

Carlos frowned.

"Juan is a common name, Papi. I know Juan Torres, Juan Pérez and Juan Rivera. They're all in my grade."

"That's true."

"We were playing 500, tossing the ball to a group of catchers while calling out a number. Juan had the best arm."

"But you've never seen this boy before?" asked Roberto.

"No, I think he's staying with the Colón's or something."

"Well, you are very fortunate to have tripped over your shoelaces," said Roberto, glancing at Carlos' shoes. "Otherwise, you would have bounced off the bumper of that speeding pickup like a pool ball. You know you're not supposed to play in West Grand."

"Papi, we always keep an eye out for cars!" protested Carlos. "And nothing happened!"

"*Nene*, nothing happened for a reason. We've told you to stay out of that street more times than I care to remember. Did Juan show up before or after you started playing?"

"He saw us in the street and asked if he could join in."

"Right. Let me tell you a story." Roberto unfastened the top button of his collared shirt.

"Many years ago, back in the 1900s, in the earlier days of Puerto Rico, there was a man named Jaime Granado."

"Papi, come on! I said I'm sorry!" protested Carlos wanting to make his dad stop with the storytelling.

"He had served honorably in the Spanish military," continued Roberto, ignoring Carlos. "And having no desire to leave the island in his middle age, he married Melchora, a creole woman. They had four daughters who were more valuable to Jaime than all the gold in Spain."

Carlos sighed.

"Now, Jaime was a man of honor and, being a member of the nobility, was aware of the priorities of the governorship. Puerto Rico was one of many Spanish colonies, but it had a poor reputation for being home to robbers and assassins. Although Jaime knew this was an exaggeration, there were, admittedly, many convicts jailed in the island's fortress.

"The King of Spain tasked the governor of Puerto Rico to 'rid the island of evils' by tackling corruption. It was customary practice for government officials to steal money from the treasury, even though Jaime had never done so. To deal with this problem, the governor ensured public officials were regularly paid. The authorities promptly brought anyone caught stealing or bribing to justice and, in most cases, sent them to the hangman.

"Jaime shared the governor's enthusiasm for order, and as his young girls grew into young adults, he became increasingly distressed at two other forms of corruption: horse racing and cockfighting. 'It is a disease that is rotting the soul of Puerto Rico!' he bemoaned. 'I cannot walk the streets of San Juan without feeling defiled! Our children are at risk.'

"Jaime voiced his concerns with his parish clergy, who acknowledged the challenges. 'We suggest you write a letter to the governor,' they said. 'Unless men of faith and virtue shed light on this darkness, what hope do we have for change?'

"Jaime, prone to flattery, took their recommendation to heart and began composing letters for the governor. He decided to send a letter once a week.

Your Grace, Lieutenant-General Miguel de la Torre, Count of Torrepando:

On behalf of the good and virtuous people of Puerto Rico, I beseech you to address the principal vices of horse racing and cockfighting, which are spreading like the plague across our land.

"He decried the foul language spilling out into the streets, the meager earnings being lost through bad bets and the all-too-persistent drinking. If he only had been more observant, he might have questioned why the clergy didn't share in his righteous anger or write letters to the governor.

"Jaime sent his letters through an errand boy, a teenage street urchin named Juan Bobo. There was no mail system like nowadays. So, every week for three months, Jaime wrote a new letter for Juan to deliver to the governor. Finally, after waiting months for an official response, Juan returned with a letter addressed to Jaime.

"'Señor, a letter for you,' said Juan, taking off his *pava* as he entered Jaime's house.

"'Bring it here, boy,' said Jaime, rising from his chair in his living room.

"Jaime opened the triangularly folded letter, his hands shaking in anticipation. He stared at the words written in cursive black ink, and his face turned crimson.

"'This is it?!' he cried at last, turning to Juan. 'This can't be. Where's the rest of it?'

"Juan held his straw hat with both hands, pressing it against his chest, but said nothing.

"'For those who gamble and are ruined, it is for the benefit of others,' read Jaime incredulously. 'How can it be *for the benefit of others?*'

"What Jamie did not realize was that the governor not only tolerated gambling in its many forms but encouraged it. He ensured cockpits were on every street corner. He sponsored carnivals to provide funding for horse tracks. And instead of revolutions, he spread diversions on the island to prevent them. The King of Spain and his vassal, the governor of Puerto Rico, could not tolerate any challenge to the Crown."

"Papi," interrupted Carlos, "haven't you always told me that cockfighting is bad? You said it was cruel."

Roberto looked gravely at his son, Carlos' eyes were wide with concern. "It's a very cruel sport," said Roberto after some time. "There's no good reason for it."

"Well, I don't like it," said Carlos.

"Neither do I. And neither did Jaime. He promised himself he would change San Juan, and by extension, the island of Puerto Rico, for the better. His anger turned into a crusade. A revolution of morality.

"In the Spring of that year, several months after Jaime received the letter from the governor, he left his home in Old San Juan and marched out into San Francisco and Cruz Streets to minister to the sinners. He started off by reading from the Gospels near the entrances of the gambling houses and cockpits during the day. He did this for two weeks, proclaiming the Word of the Lord until his voice went hoarse.

"By the third week, he noticed the crowds increased in the evenings, prompting him to camp in the plaza to preach the Gospel through the night and sleep during the day.

"His wife Melchora and their four daughters were aghast at Jaime's behavior. He was living like a vagrant, sleeping with rats and drunks. They implored him to come home, to let the issue go. They warned him of the danger of those streets.

"'Jamie, those streets are the Devil's playground!' cried Melchora.

"'Papá, there are villains on every corner!' said one of his daughters.

"'Some are murderers and thieves!' said another daughter.

"Jaime was unmoved. He erected a simple log lean-to against a palm tree and had no plans to leave. In desperation, Melchora called for Juan Bobo.

"'You must go bring him home. I beg of you,' implored Melchora. 'You know the ways of the street. You will keep him safe.'

"'Señora, on my honor, I will bring him home,' said Juan, making the sign of the cross before turning to leave his master's house.

"That night, there were huge crowds at the gambling houses and cockpits on San Fransisco and Cruz Streets. Men squeezed past each other, shoulder to shoulder, to make their wagers on two gamecocks—one owned by a local peasant family and the other by the island's secretary of finance. These ferocious birds had torn apart their rivals in matches throughout the year. The secretary of finance had a large, powerful rooster, while the peasant family had a quick, accurate striker. Many people placed their money on the secretary of finance's rooster, but they all wanted the peasant's gamecock to win.

"Except Jaime.

"'Why are these crowds here?' asked a haggard-looking Jaime, grasping the shoulder of a man walking toward one of the cockpits.

"'Get your hand off me, you crazy fool,' said the man, smelling of beer. 'Don't you know?'

"But Jaime didn't know because he wasn't paying attention to the street activity. He had spent so much time focused on his revolution that he had forgotten how to look and listen.

"'These crowds are here because of the two prizefighters going against each other tonight,' said Juan, appearing by his side. 'One is owned by the Romero family, and the other by Don Jomar, the secretary of finance.'

"'The secretary of finance?' asked Jaime, staring blankly at the boy by his side.

"'Yes, Señor,' said Juan. 'This is the fight of the year. The whole city is talking about it.'

"'The secretary of finance?' Jaime repeated in disbelief. 'The government official in charge of public funds?'

"'It is as you say,' said Juan.

"'The secretary of finance is conspiring with these people?'

"'That is one way to look at it, Señor.'

"'What other ways are there to look at it?' demanded Jaime, his voice rising. 'What kind of fool do you think I am?'

"Jaime glanced at a wooden crate lying flat on the ground a few feet away, near a brick wall, and stepped on top of it. The sea of men moving in and out of the gambling houses and cockpits seemed to stop in their tracks, when Jaime lifted his Bible into the air and bellowed, "'This evil needs to stop! Shame on you! Shame on you!'

"He glared at the assembly of people. Sweat poured down his face. He panted.

"The crowd erupted. Cheers rang out. Men cursed. People waved pieces of paper. Gamblers swarmed around Juan.

"'Take my ticket. I had six to one on him doing that!' yelled one.

"'I had five to one!' yelled another.

"'I knew today would be the day!' said another.

"People exchanged paper tickets for cash. Men howled in laughter, patting Jaime's boots as they ambled into the cockpits. Songs broke out. Some people shook their fists at him. One man peed on his crate.

"At last, when the streets were quiet, and the gamblers and revelers were indoors, watching the fights or playing cards or dominoes, Jaime did not move. He stood on the crate, with the Bible by his side, blinking. Juan was strumming his *cuatro* a couple of feet away.

"'I can't believe it. Have I been used as an instrument of corruption all this time?' Jaime asked.

"'Yes, Señor. You've become a person of interest on these streets. You're like a prizefighter.'

"'A prizefighter?'

"'Yes, Señor,' said Juan. 'There was a lot of money on you this evening. You did extremely well.'

"'I attracted gamblers?' said Jaime.

"'You were the opening act, Señor,' said Juan. 'The word on the street is that the governor and his men placed a lot of money on you. You made many people happy.'

"The following week, while Jaime was still asleep, and the sun had barely reached above the clouds, Melchora met Juan outside her home. In her hands, she held a small leather satchel.

"'This is for you,' she said, handing him the bag. 'You should have no trouble eating for the next year.'

"'God bless you, Señora.'

"'No, God bless you,' she said. 'I still don't know how you brought him home.'

"'Certain things that are better left unsaid,' said Juan.

"'Jaime has sworn to never preach again,' she said. 'He wants to return to Spain, but I know he's not serious. He doesn't like traveling by sea.'

"'Perhaps he will spend more time at home?' said Juan.

"'That's my hope,' she said. 'You have saved my marriage, Juan Bobo. You have saved Jaime from beatings. From death by disease. You have rescued him from the streets.'

"And from that day forward, as Jaime recovered his health and his senses, he became a more dutiful husband, an attentive father and a man who rarely left his home other than to attend Sunday Mass."

Roberto looked at Carlos, who was sitting on the edge of his seat. A soft whisper of a breeze brushed past Roberto, as a figure in a hat flashed by him.

"Papi," said Carlos at last, "you're right. I had never seen that boy before. He came out of nowhere, like a spirit."

"These things happen."

"I felt like I was pushed or tripped on the sidewalk near the speeding truck."

"The driver had blown through a stop sign," added Roberto.

"That street is dangerous," said Carlos.

"Yes, very dangerous."

"I think we'll play ball somewhere else from now on."

Roberto smiled and placed his hand on Carlos' shoulder

"I bought a six-pack of Coke on the way home," said Roberto, pointing to a paper bag on the porch floor. "Let's go inside and have some while they're still cold. Tomorrow, I'll show you a nice field where you can play without scratching your elbows and knees, or worse. And remember, if you ever need a strong arm, I'm here."

"Thank you, Papi. I'd like that."

THE WOMAN HE HOPED TO LOVE

It was an ephemeral sort of love. A passing shower. A brief interlude. But it left a mark all the same. A love that grew from the dengue fever Luis Burgos had just recovered from, a bone-crushing sickness that shook him to his core.

Some people say you're unlucky if you get a bad case of dengue the first time. If you get it a second time, you're dead — or perhaps, you're lucky to be dead. It's all a matter of perspective.

Luis had contracted the virus shortly after returning from a trip to the island. He had flown with his father to Guaynabo to help make repairs to his grandparents' home following Hurricane Hugo. He had spent days working outside in T-shirts and shorts. He felt achy and tired on the flight back to Chicago but thought little of it. Given the long days spent clearing trees, planting coco plum and plantain, and constructing a new veranda, the weariness he felt at home didn't compare. The fever hit him the day after he returned from Puerto Rico right before he was supposed to work at the restaurant.

Luis had a piercing migraine, feeling it behind his eyes and was sick to his stomach and clammy. He had no energy to rise from bed, and when his mother entered his bedroom

49

to check on him, he could make out her taut expression and knew something was wrong.

"You're burning up," she said, removing her hand from his forehead and leaving the room. Soon, she was back with Ibuprofen and a small glass of milk. She lifted Luis' head to help administer the pills, but the smell of the milk caused him to vomit.

A couple hours later, when his temperature had reached 104° and he had developed a rash on his stomach, his mother called for an ambulance. "They're taking you to Humboldt Park Health," she said, holding his hand while they carried him on a stretcher to the vehicle outside.

What happened next was a blur. Luis recalled the movement of the ambulance, its flashing lights, and the men in surgical masks, but most of all, he felt heavy. He felt like he was being squeezed, and his insides were being crushed.

At one point, he saw an IV line. He thought it was a snake. It slithered along his arm, tongue flicking, as it coiled around his shoulder and toward his neck and chest. "There'ssss no ressssissssing," it hissed.

Luis stared at its scaly brown face. Its eyes were darker than the darkest night.

Minutes blended into hours, hours into lifetimes.

"I've taken otherssss in your tree," it taunted. "Rossssario, before her fifth birthday. Nicolassss, the old *machetero*."

Luis shuddered. These names were unfamiliar, yet the words stung as if he had lost a brother or sister.

Luis thought about all the things he still wanted to do. The restaurant he wished to open. The cities he planned to see. The woman he hoped to love.

These thoughts filled him with sadness. *So many missed opportunities*, he said to himself. *So little time....*

He thought about his sister, Ofelia, and regretted teasing her about her glasses in front of his friends. He thought of his father, Roberto, and regretted not waking when he woke, not making him coffee, not showing greater gratitude for working such spirit-crushing jobs. He thought about his knee, how he blew it out, and how he would never reach his potential in baseball. He also regretted not asking Camila to walk with him that night. Now, it was too late and she was engaged.

He thought about the past week spent in Guaynabo and regretted not listening to his grandmother, who had told him to wear long sleeves and pants. He regretted not wearing insect repellent. He regretted not knocking over buckets of standing water. He regretted causing his mother to miss work. He regretted causing his family to worry. He regretted being in this room.

The coils tightening around him, and his breathing became labored. He was slipping into the blackest of blackest nights.

Suddenly a memory of his mother flashed in his mind. He recalled how she dabbed his eyes after he fell from his skateboard. She told him to get back up and try again. She stood on it herself, despite never having stood on a skateboard before, to show him it was okay. She demonstrated how to face his fear of falling and prove to him that time is too short for fears to stop our joy.

And he remembered how he listened and followed her example. With a scraped knee and scratched elbow, he got back up. With his heart racing, he got back up. With his mind second-guessing, he got back up. With his mother looking on and smiling, he got back up.

"Because that is what we do," his mother said. "That is what the Burgos family does. We don't stay down. We get back up and fight until we have nothing left to give. Until the last embers fade into smoke."

In the distance, a form took shape. It was long and slender, with short legs, light brown fur and a long tail. It trotted up to Luis, sniffing the air with its pointy snout.

A mongoose thought Luis. *I have seen you before among the grasses. Once even on the steps of my grandparents' house, while they played* danzas *from Juan Morel Campos on the record player.*

The mongoose looked at Luis, then turned to the constrictor and stood up on its hind legs, as if waiting for its partner for a ballroom dance. The constrictor released its grip on Luis and slid toward the mongoose, rising in front of it, ready to make its move.

Luis thought he could hear the tinny sound of the *cuatro*, strumming a waltz. As the music became more distinct, the constrictor and the mongoose began their syncopated dance. The mongoose feinted a swipe of its paw at the constrictor, which lunged at the mongoose with its hooked teeth. But the mongoose was too quick, and the constrictor's teeth only brushed its fur. The mongoose dodged another swipe, moving in a clockwise motion, with the constrictor attempting to strike it once more, but to no avail. Again the mongoose darted forward and backward, from side to side, just out of reach of the furious constrictor. They spun and spun, the *cuatro* playing to three-four time, the music increasing in urgency, faster and faster, louder and louder, until the constrictor was wobbling and the mongoose, seeing its opportunity, pounced and sunk its teeth into the back of the reptile's head while the constrictor writhed on the ground and was finally still.

Luis opened his eyes suddenly and inhaled deeply, the bright lights of the hospital ward jolting him upright. At his side, he saw a nurse removing the IV line from his arm and applying pressure to the insertion site with gauze.

"There now," she said, placing tape over the gauze and skin and nuzzling his head back onto his pillow.

Luis stared at her, blinking, as his eyes regained focus. *Is this an angel?* he thought. He looked at her tall and slender frame. Her light brown hair cascaded down her shoulders and over her blue scrubs. *Is this real?*

"You have been asleep for nearly forty-eight hours," she said, adjusting the IV pole.

"But I've seen you before, haven't I?" asked Luis.

The nurse looked at Luis, curious. Her hazel eyes were like sargassum floating in a gently undulating pool. Her lips were like a mother-of-pearl. "Have you?" she asked.

Luis thought about the mongoose, but his memory was fading. The dreams were slipping back to the shadowlands. *What was it I just saw?* he asked himself.

"You're fortunate," said the nurse. "You could have gone into shock. Dengue is a dangerous disease."

"Dengue?"

"Yes, the physician will be in soon," she said. "He will explain."

The nurse left the room, and Luis lay staring at the ceiling for some time. He was tired but not weak. He felt strong, and his mind was now filled with new dreams—dreams that take place during the day. Dreams of a woman playing the *cuatro* by his side. Dreams of her fingers dancing along the frets, darting up and down to a waltz that pumped blood through his veins. Dreams of the woman he hoped to love.

When the physician entered the room with Luis' mother and father and spoke of him being discharged in a day or two, if all went well, it filled Luis with gratitude. He was grateful they had stood by his side and giving him the strength to fight the suffocating sickness. But most of all, he thought about her and how even the tiniest ember of hope could shine through the darkest regrets and, if nurtured just right, could burst into something more.

THE SABOTEUR

Ofelia Burgos was 35 years old, single, slightly chubby and very angry. She wasn't normally angry. In fact, most of her family members, friends and acquaintances would describe her as calm and composed, even unflappable.

She was a Capricorn, the embodiment of maturity, and although she didn't believe in astrology, she accepted this zodiac trait as a fact. She made good decisions, such as studying nursing and later getting a Ph.D. in public health. This was a first in the Burgos family, leading her to RTI International, based in North Carolina, where she served as a consultant and expert in maternal health issues.

She was remarkably attentive to details and organized to a fault. These attributes helped her advance in her career, and she was highly sought-after in both industry and government clients for her research and insights. Her steely determination to get her way on issues that really mattered to her was not lost on those who knew her. It was what made her successful. It was also, coincidentally, what made her single.

Her stature, which was only five feet one inch, may have been a contributing factor to her single status as well. She had thick, dark-brown hair shaped into a short, choppy bob that commanded respect. Her leopard-patterned cat-eye-glasses added an extra element of sophistication and fun, except when she was angry.

And she was angry now. Irate. And groggy. And disoriented.

She was sitting on the edge of a double bed in the Ritz-Carlton in Georgetown. She had no knowledge of checking into this room (although she did, in principle, approve of the Ritz-Carlton). She was still wearing a white jersey dress. Her black blazer was folded neatly in half on the other side of the bed, along with her woven black high-heel mules. She had a splitting headache, and the exterior light penetrating the room from the oversized windows was not helping.

In the middle of her bed, there was a large yellow stain. She touched her lower back, and it was wet.

Across from her, on the second double bed, sat a black-and-tan, rough-coated Brussels Griffon with prominent whiskers and a noticeable underbite. It was not her dog. She had never seen it before. It was sitting on its hind legs, staring at her curiously, expectantly, through its small, beady brown eyes.

This was odd but did not upset her. The dog blinked an eye and tilted its head, causing its lower left canine to pop out over its lip. She noticed it had no tag and no obvious form of identification on its collar.

Her suitcase was open on the floor in between the beds. A moment earlier, she had rummaged through it, and although most of her belongings were there, her speaker notes for her keynote speech at the International Conference on Public Health were missing. This upset her. Nearly ten pages of them had been handwritten, meticulously scribed with different colored pens to emphasize critical points in her speech.

But what upset her most was the call from her co-workers ten minutes ago.

"Ofelia, finally! We've been trying to reach you," said Chloe Choi. "I have you on speakerphone. We're at the Ronald Reagan Building in the cafeteria. The oral presentation is in forty minutes. Is everything okay? Will you be able to get here on time?"

"Chloe?" asked Ofelia, still half asleep.

"Jesus," said Mathew Parker in the background," she sounds out of it."

"Are you okay, Ofelia?" asked Chloe. "Where are you? We lost track of you last night."

"You missed our nightcap," said Everly O'Brien. "We were in the JW Marriott lobby last evening."

Then it dawned on her. It was Monday, July 21, 8:50 a.m. She was the lead presenter to USAID for an oral presentation. The presentation was to be recorded, and there were strict limits on their time with the government contracting officials. This was one of the largest opportunities of the year. Unfortunately for Ofelia, she was in the wrong hotel, on the wrong side of town, and had less than forty minutes to get there.

This made her angry. She was never late. She always dressed impeccably. She was always focused, well-prepared and ready to perform when it mattered. It was her brand.

She rose to her feet and staggered to the bathroom. She walked into a separate vanity area with exquisite white Italian marble countertops. She grazed her hand against a plush terrycloth robe hanging from a wall rack and noticed a spacious soaking tub and stall shower in an adjoining room. There was a luxury Asprey Purple Water travel set next to the sink, featuring a blend of orange and jacaranda flowers, lemon, mandarin and ginger essential oils. Ofelia thought, *I don't know what the heck is going on, but I definitely need to book another stay at the Ritz.*

She placed her hands on the countertop and inspected herself by leaning into the wall-mounted vanity mirror. Amazingly, the subsequent scream woke the nearby guests without shattering any glass.

A few minutes later, the landline rang in her room.

"Good morning, Dr. Burgos," said the concierge. "I trust you're doing well and enjoying your stay?"

"What, um, yes, yes, the hotel is marvelous." *At least, what I've seen of it,* she thought.

"That's great to hear. There was a report of a disturbance, and we wanted to make sure everything was okay?"

Ofelia sighed. "Candidly, no, things are *not* entirely okay. My hair is a disaster. A shocking, frizzy mess. And I'm running late for a presentation. Could you arrange a cab?"

In the rush to leave for the Ronald Reagan Building, she hadn't changed. She brush her teeth, shaped her hair into place to the best of her ability, applied blush and eyeliner, sprayed deodorant, grabbed her briefcase with her laptop and slipped on her blazer. She was on her way out, unsteadily running through her checklist of to-dos in the center of the room, when she saw the dog sitting on its hind legs in front of the entry door with its leash in its mouth.

"Er, so listen, doggie," said Ofelia, freezing, "this isn't the best time for a walk."

The Brussels Griffon cocked its head and slid its wiry tail slowly back and forth on the carpet. The dog reminded her of an Ewok from *Star Wars*.

"Oh...well...*¡Coño!*" she growled, reverting to Spanish, as was her habit when frustrated.

Outside, under the black metal hotel awning, Ofelia stood waiting for the cab, her briefcase in one hand and the dog leash in the other. It was 9:05 a.m., and her brain fog was beginning to fade. She desperately needed a coffee.

At 9:07 a.m., a DC Yellow Cab pulled up (ironically, it was painted red with a gray swoosh on the side doors). As the driver stepped out of the car to help with her bag, she felt a warm trickle on her left foot. The dog had its right hind leg hiked as it looked up at her, blinking, appearing forlorn as it squirted one last full stream before emptying its bladder.

"Seriously?" she cried. "Well, now I *know* you're a guy! A girl would never be this obnoxious!"

"I'm sorry," said the cab driver. "I thought you might need help with your bags. I didn't mean to express some sort of medieval chivalry. Women shouldn't be held to different standards than men, shouldn't be treated differently, like they can't take care of themselves."

"What?" she asked, her mouth open before shaking it off. "Yeah, right, that kind of thing. Would you happen to have a tissue?"

Traffic was mercifully light on the Whitehurst Freeway. The cab was making good progress, and she thought she might just make it to the Ronald Reagan Building in time.

She glanced at the Potomac River from her passenger seat window, then shut her eyes. *I need to collect myself,* she thought. *Okay, I have A LOT of questions, but I need to focus on this presentation.* She stroked the dog on her lap absentmindedly and began rehearsing. *There are several key factors influencing maternal and child morbidity and mortality in these regions of Peru. We see this project as a catalyst that will support Peru, to deliver sustainable improvements in health outcomes, particularly for its most vulnerable women.*

The car lurched to a stop, and her briefcase ricocheted off the back of the driver's seat to the floor. She was cradling the dog protectively, and they were nose-to-nose.

"And you can go to hell, you bastard!" shouted the driver, leaning out of the window and rocking his fist. "Tourists. They just don't get it."

"Okie dokie," said Ofelia under her breath while adjusting the dog on her lap.

Five minutes later, they pulled in behind a Loudoun County commuter bus at the 14th Street entrance to USAID's headquarters. It was 9:24 a.m. and, against her better judgment, she needed to ask the driver for a favor.

"So, I'm in a massive hurry," she began. "Any chance you could wait for me? I can't bring the dog with me. It's a long story. Let's just say he won't pass security."

"I'm going to have to charge you extra for the dog," said the driver, "but look, missus, if you pay, I'll stay."

Ofelia stepped out of the cab and speed-walked to the entrance. When she entered the building, Everly was waiting for her in the lobby near the security checkpoint. Pacing back and forth, she sighed dramatically when she saw her.

"Ofelia, you certainly know how to make a grand entrance!"

Ofelia nodded and hurriedly tossed her briefcase onto the baggage conveyor. "Good morning, Everly."

"Chloe and Mathew are already in the conference room," said Everly, watching the briefcase go through the X-ray machine. "They're setting up our laptop for the presentation. I was ready to present in your absence. Thank goodness you're here."

"We need to revisit our company's policy about having senior managers leading customer presentations. Otherwise, you would do a great job," said Ofelia.

The presentation was held in a sixth-floor conference room large enough to fit about twenty people. The main table had name tent cards placed to each USAID official, who were seated and waiting for Ofelia and Everly to arrive. There were seven government officials seated at one end of the table, across from the RTI International team. Ms. Henderson, the senior USAID contracting officer, a wizened, angular, elderly woman with a perpetual frown, gray curly hair and rimless reading spectacles, sat in the center of the USAID group with her arms crossed over her brown cardigan sweater.

Ofelia and Everly stepped into the conference room with a few seconds to spare and sat down between Mathew and Chloe. The title slide of their PowerPoint presentation was projected on the wall-mounted TV, and Mathew held a remote control in his hand, ready to navigate the slides.

"We're all set up and ready to go," said Chloe, handing Ofelia a Starbucks Grande latte. "I thought you might need this."

Ofelia gratefully took the cup, pulling the green plastic splash stick out of the lid. "You're a lifesaver," she said, taking a quick sip, then promptly spraying it out of her mouth and across the table. "So sorry, that's very hot!"

She glanced at Mr. Wilkinson, seated to the right of Ms. Henderson. He was a middle-aged man with a receding hairline, dressed in a navy blue blazer and slacks, a white button-down shirt and a red-and-blue striped silk tie. Tan coffee spots splattered his notepad.

"Well, then," Ofelia said sheepishly, "shall we get started?"

We all have days when the dominoes fall in a neat line, according to design, and we feel like architects of our destiny. Take, for example, a well-planned family vacation to the beach. You've been planning this trip for months, researching the best time to head out before the roads become congested. You find the perfect bed-and-breakfast just a short walk from the boardwalk and make reservations with the best restaurants in town.

The dominoes had fallen prematurely and unevenly, and Ofelia, despite her best efforts, could not seem to grab destiny by the shirt collar. The main issue was that she was still drowsy. The brain fog hadn't fully cleared. It was like a hangover that just wouldn't give up.

There was no doubt that she understood the intent of USAID's Request for Proposal. Her company's written proposal, which she had helped draft and submit, was strong, and they had won similar work with USAID in other parts of the world. But an oral presentation is a performance, and she struggled with the Xs and Os. Specifically, she was struggling with focusing and maintaining her train of thought.

"Let me ask you this question again, maybe slightly differently and more directly this time," said Ms. Henderson impatiently. "How does RTI International plan to improve maternal health services in Peru? How do you plan to work with local partners to achieve this goal?"

"Ah, yes. Happy to elaborate," said Ofelia, taking off her blazer and placing it on her lap. "It's a bit stuffy here, is it not?" She wiped away a bead of sweat from her forehead with the back of her hand. "You see, we take a whole-system approach to designing health programs. We look at the full condominium of care to ensure local stakeholder ownership."

"I think you meant..." started Mathew.

"You provide health care in multi-tenant housing?" interjected Ms. Henderson.

"I don't see how condominiums are relevant to this discussion," said Mr. Wilkinson.

"What? Oh, no, I said *continuum*."

"I distinctly heard you say condominium," countered Mr. Wilkinson.

"Well, we can agree to disagree."

Chloe nudged Ofelia on the shoulder. That's not how this works, she whispered. "We want them to *agree* with us."

"As I was saying," Ofelia continued, "we have a wealth of experience delivering..." Ofelia stared at her coffee cup as if trying to summon the remaining caffeine to activate her brain. The green-and-white design reminded her of Christmas packaging. "We have a wealth of experience delivering holiday packages."

There was an awkward silence, and Everly and Ms. Henderson exchanged looks.

"We don't actually deliver holiday packages," said Everly eventually.

"Yes, I assumed this to be another misunderstanding."

A little past 10:00 a.m., Ofelia, Mathew, Chloe and Everly stood in the hallway waiting for the elevator to take them downstairs. Ofelia held her briefcase in one hand, her blazer folded over her other arm.

"So, that went, um, reasonably well," said Chloe. "I mean, it could have, theoretically, been worse."

"It was an unmitigated disaster," said Mathew, staring at the ceiling tiles, his hands on his hips.

"We all have our highs and lows," contributed Everly.

"That's right," added Chloe. "What's important is that we learn and adjust accordingly."

The elevator opened and out came a party of three women. At the head of the group was someone around the same age as Ofelia, but several inches taller. She had long blond hair that fell over the padded shoulders of her cropped, pink houndstooth blazer. A subtle aroma of jasmine and rose essence wafted through the air.

"What a surprise!" she exclaimed, pushing her oversized aviator sunglasses up the bridge of her nose, even though there was little risk of sun glare. "Team RTI! And Dr. Ofelia Burgos, the crème de la crème of our industry. What a pleasure to see you!"

"Good morning, Dr. Julia Jennings," said Ofelia, less enthusiastically. "Are we to assume that you're here for the oral presentations as well?"

"As a matter of fact, we are," she replied with an air of supreme confidence. "Chemonics is a uniquely trusted partner with USAID, and we certainly couldn't pass up the opportunity. It's the nature of this business." She glanced at Ofelia's dress and stepped forward, bending slightly to examine the backside. "Oh dear, I hate to say this in front of the group, but since we're all professional colleagues... you *are* aware, I *assume*, that you have a large yellow stain on the back of your dress? Such a beautiful outfit, I must add. What a shame."

Julia's two coworkers, standing behind her, locked eyes with each other and half-heartedly attempted to suppress a laugh. Julia looked at Ofelia with feigned concern.

"Oh yes, there is a story to tell..." started Ofelia, unfurling her blazer, and slipping it on.

"Well, we'll be going on now," said Chloe hurriedly, hooking her arm into Ofelia's arm and pulling her into the elevator. "We don't want to hold you up. Best of luck!"

Julia smiled broadly, her white teeth gleaming, edged with a pronounced smugness.

"We must catch up at the conference tomorrow," called Julia as the elevator door shut. "I can't wait to hear your keynote and learn more about your wild weekend at the Ritz."

Ofelia's cab, which had been circling the Ronald Reagan Building for the past fifteen minutes, pulled to the curb near the 14th Street entrance shortly after Ofelia exited. The sky was turning gray, and the damp air was warm and discomforting. Mathew and Everly, who lived in Northern Virginia and had carpooled together into the city, had left for the parking garage. Chloe was walking beside Ofelia on her way to the JW Marriott, where she was staying.

"So, what was that all about? The wild weekend and all? The Ritz?"

Ofelia waved at the cab driver and saw the little black-and-tan dog peeking its head out the open passenger window.

"That's an excellent question, Chloe. I have no idea what she was talking about. When was the last time you saw me?"

"At dinner last night, at 1789. You remember, don't you? We were all there."

"That's right," said Ofelia, rubbing her temples. "I do remember. They served a lovely brioche-crusted halibut."

"So… what's going on?"

"Hold that thought."

Ofelia walked over to the cab. The dog began wagging its tail excitedly. It was standing on its hind legs with its front paws resting on the interior door panel.

"I just need ten minutes," Ofelia said to the driver, reaching through the passenger-side window and pulling out the dog with its leash. The dog reminded her of an extra-large Brillo pad, which was growing on her.

"Have you ever seen this guy before?" asked Ofelia as she approached her. They were standing next to the Oscar S. Straus Memorial Fountain.

Chloe stared for a moment at the dog sniffing her heels, then shook her head. "Never. Whose dog is it?"

"It was in my room when I woke up this morning. Coincidentally, I had no recollection of checking into the Ritz. I booked a room at the JW Marriott. A stay at the Ritz is way too expensive for company reimbursement."

"Let me get this straight," said Chloe incredulously. "You have no recollection of checking into the Ritz-Carlton, where you stayed last night. You have no recollection of this dog, which is in your possession. Do you even know its name?"

"I just call it Doggie," said Ofelia.

"Right. We need to work on that. Anyway, you have no recollection of checking into the Ritz, no idea where this dog came from, and you nearly missed orals today. Strange. Very strange."

"That about sums it up."

Chloe rubbed her chin. "You're not having a secret love affair?"

"Not to my knowledge. Which is disappointing, let me assure you of that. I would be happily involved in a secret love affair if I was in on the secret."

Chloe's eyes widened and she gasped, "You don't think someone drugged you, do you?"

"That definitely crossed my mind."

"And that someone took advantage of you…"

"Could be. Although unlikely, given that I was fully clothed this morning, and there was a dog in the neighboring bed. But we can't rule out the possibility."

"Oh God," cried Chloe, sitting abruptly on the fountain ledge.

"Hey, no need to panic," said Ofelia, patting Chloe on the shoulder. "The circumstances are very unusual. I don't think *that* happened. You see, I noticed something else that was odd."

Ofelia sat down next to Chloe and began rubbing the dog's belly.

"I noticed that my conference speaker notes were gone. I searched the entire room. If I were to make an educated guess, someone's out to sabotage me. Think about it. You and

I fly to DC from Raleigh-Durham this weekend. The night before the oral presentation, I'm drugged. I nearly missed our meeting because I'm staying on the other side of town. I have some mysterious dog in my room, which I have to attend to because, well, it would be wrong not to take care of it. Doggie further complicates my ability to get out of the hotel room on time for our meeting. My detailed speaker notes, which I've handwritten, are gone the day before my keynote. Oh, and our USAID technical evaluation committee, including Ms. Henderson herself, are all planning to attend tomorrow's conference."

"Could it be Julia Jennings? She wouldn't dare!"

"She seemed uniquely aware of my stay at the Ritz."

Ofelia stood up and stared at the white USAID flag fluttering in the wind. A slight breeze was picking up, hinting at an afternoon shower. "There's only one way to find out. I'm heading back to the Ritz."

"Hey, don't leave without me! We're in this together."

If luxury was a distraction for the uninitiated, then the Ritz-Carlton's lobby lounge was a diversion of the first order. Having grown up in inner-city Chicago and later having spent much of her career traveling the developing world on humanitarian missions, Ofelia wasn't used to pampering and opulence. Granted, she'd been looking forward to staying at the JW Marriott, which was an attractive hotel but this boutique hotel, nestled in the heart of Georgetown in a refurbished industrial building, oozed glamor and refinement. The lounge featured floor-to-ceiling windows lined with bronze-colored, side-swept curtains that darkened the space to create an air of intimacy. Jewel-toned furnishings, elaborate flower arrangements and custom sectionals and armchairs contrasted with the bare brick walls.

Chloe was sitting cross-legged on a stool beside the bar, dangling her black stiletto toward a man a couple of seats away while sipping a French Martini. She wore a navy blue, form-fitting blazer dress and appeared more at home in the Ritz-Carlton than in any government building. She was staring alluringly at the businessman, whose back was slightly turned to her, when Ofelia walked over with the dog and interrupted her advances.

"Oh yes, Ofelia, what did you learn?" she frowned.

Ofelia plopped down on the barstool between Chloe and the businessman and shook her head. "The room is booked under my name through tonight, but it was pre-paid by an anonymous benefactor."

"Did they provide any other details? Who physically checked you in?"

"I checked myself in. But I was accompanied by a man."

"You're kidding!" hissed Chloe. "What did he look like?"

"Well, they said he was tall. Over six feet. With a dark complexion. Brown, tousled, curly hair, with a five-o'clock shadow, and dressed in a business suit."

Ofelia and Chloe turned slowly toward the man next to them. The Brussels Griffon was licking the man's black dress shoes.

"Ahem," said Ofelia. "Ahem, sir."

Ofelia noticed he was wearing wireless AirPods and was engrossed in a copy of the *Financial Times*. She tapped him on his shoulder, and he jumped out of his seat in surprise, knocking over his glass and spilling water on his newspaper.

"Ofelia!" he exclaimed, whirling around and pulling his AirPods from his ears. "Oh my goodness, I am so sorry. I didn't see you there. How are you?"

"Um, well, I'm fine, I suppose…" she began.

"Boris!" he cried, picking up the dog, whose tail was wagging. "I am *so* grateful to you. I was out all last night, and Boris gets so scared by himself. Thank you *so* much for watching him. I hope it wasn't too much of an inconvenience."

Ofelia looked at Chloe and she waved at the bartender, who was delivering cocktails to a couple sitting in one of the sectionals in the lounge. "Okay, so, I don't mean to be rude, but who are you?"

The man's expression changed, and he appeared crestfallen. "We spoke for at least an hour last night, before I had to go to the ER."

"Doesn't ring a bell," replied Ofelia. She then turned to the bartender and ordered a drink like Chloe's. "I'll take one of those. And please don't hold back on the vodka."

"Me too. Another, please," added Chloe.

"Oh, God. This is awkward," said the man, rubbing the back of his head. "I'm Kendrick. We spoke last evening in the lobby. Remember we were discussing Chicago?"

"No, I'm sorry, I don't remember."

"I grew up in Sauganash. I've been to your brother's café in Oak Park. I think you said his name was Luis?"

"Did I?" She responded hesitantly.

Kendrick looked embarrassed; his handsome features contorted in pain. His tan skin was becoming a shade of red. "I live in Reston and I'm attending the International Conference on Public Health tomorrow. Unfortunately, I was on call and had to rush back to Reston last night to provide emergency surgery. I had hoped to get away for a couple of days without interruption."

"So, you're a surgeon?" asked Chloe, twirling her long black ponytail. "And are you single?"

"Yes, I'm a general surgeon. Work has been so consuming, and I haven't had time for a committed relationship," he said

"I feel the same," bemoaned Ofelia.

"I know. We spoke about that last evening!" Kendrick said, meeting Ofelia's eyes.

She couldn't help but notice his broad shoulders and captivating eyes. *He does have nice broad shoulders. And those eyes...* Ofelia thought.

"You didn't escort me to my room last night?" she asked, a hint of curiosity in her tone. "With the dog, of course."

"I'm afraid not. But I walked with you to the front desk to check in." He responded, squashing any notions of a romantic escapade. Ofelia couldn't help but express her disappointment humorously. *Well, that eliminates any secret love affair,* she thought.

"You don't seem to remember much of our conversation, do you?" he observed. "I had to rush off. I handed you Boris, at this bar. Again, I can't thank you enough for your kindness and generosity. And Boris seems quite fond of you."

"Kendrick, would you mind describing your conversation with Ofelia last night?" asked Chloe, who had been standing nearby listening to their conversation.

The bartender placed two martinis on the table. "Better make that three," Kendrick said to him. "Ofelia, you appeared a bit tipsy last night, now that I think about it. But nothing out of the ordinary, " he said, stroking Boris, who was curled in a ball on his lap.

"I was having a drink at the bar when I saw you enter the lobby. A group of people were standing nearby. They'd been there for a while and were on their way out when you arrived. You started talking to a blonde-haired woman, and the conversation became a bit animated. I heard you mention something about a night out on the town and a keynote. A few minutes later, you came over to the bar and ordered a Moscow Mule. You mentioned something about needing a vacation, and we got to talking. I learned you were from Chicago, and we started talking about all the places we'd like to go. Then my cell phone rang, and I had to leave."

Chloe leaned into Ofelia's ear. "Julia!" She whispered.

"Did you see me holding anything? A folder?"

"No, not that I recall."

"Where could my notes have gone?" muttered Ofelia.

"I'm sorry?"

"Oh, nothing," Ofelia said. "I just seemed to have lost something."

"Ofelia's the keynote speaker at the conference tomorrow," said Chloe, nibbling on a raspberry skewered on a plastic cocktail pick. "But her speaker notes have vanished."

"That's unfortunate," said Kendrick.

The bartender placed a martini next to Kendrick, which he sipped before offering an idea. "Why don't you do a dry run with me tonight?"

"Oh no, I couldn't..." Ofelia protested.

"Really, it would be my pleasure."

"It's been a whirlwind," Ofelia said.

"Over dinner?" Kendrick suggested. "Perhaps with a good Côtes du Rhône?"

"That's not how I typically prepare..."

"Okay, that's enough," Chloe interrupted. "Yes, she'd love to. She'll meet you here at 7:00 p.m. sharp. In the meantime, let's find those notes of yours, Ofelia."

A short while later, Ofelia and Chloe were in the one-bedroom suite of the Ritz-Carlton. Ofelia was reclining on a plush, striped, brown-and-tan sofa in the living room with her hands behind her head. Her high heels were lying nearby on the floor. Chloe was on her knees, looking under the box spring in the adjacent room. She tossed pineapple-patterned pajama shorts over her shoulder toward the French doors.

"Those are my favorite bottoms!"

"I've looked everywhere," said Chloe, brushing lint off her suit dress as she stood up. "There is no sign of speaker notes."

Ofelia sighed. "I'll just have to make do without them."

Chloe entered the living room and sank into a leather armchair across from Ofelia. "Well, you probably don't need them, anyway. Everly's always talking about how she was a debate club champion, and never used notes." She put her feet up on the glass-top coffee table and stared dreamily at the wall.

"When was the last time you went on a date?" asked Chloe after a minute.

"You mean, like with Kendrick? No, we're not having a date," replied Ofelia.

"Yes, you're definitely having a date. It's pretty much the definition of a date."

"He's just helping me prepare for my speech. And, by the way, maybe Doggie, er, Boris ate my speaker notes. You never know with those terrier-like dogs."

"He did seem rather fit…"

"All right!" exclaimed Ofelia, sitting upright. "Let me ask you something. Did you see me take a cab from the restaurant to the Ritz last night?"

However, Chloe was staring at the wall and did not reply.

"Hello, Earth to Chloe," Ofelia said, waving her hand back and forth.

"What?" Chloe exhaled deeply.

"No, I didn't see you take a cab after dinner last night," replied Chloe. "After we paid our bill, I went to the restroom.

You were already on your way out with Everly and Mathew. I remember you rushing to finish your wine. Maybe it went to your head."

"I do remember having an exquisite Chardonnay."

"You must have taken a taxi."

"Speaking of Chardonnay, are you planning to attend the networking event this afternoon?"

"I thought about going. Generally, I don't pass up free drinks and hors d'oeuvres."

"And Chemonics, no doubt, will be there?"

"Julia Jennings is an insufferable socialite."

"Right. I have an idea."

"Uh oh. I'm not sure I like where this is going."

"Nothing to worry about," said Ofelia, standing up. "Just a little investigative work while we do some networking. Connecting the dots, so to speak."

The networking event was held at the National Press Club, which was also the venue for the conference. Ofelia and Chloe arrived a little after 3:00 p.m. and followed the signs to the First Amendment Lounge, a large, blue-carpeted room with a mahogany bar and floor-to-ceiling windows offering views of the White House and the Washington Monument. There were several dozen people gathered in the room when Ofelia and Chloe arrived, with most people milling about catering tables like ants drawn to sugar.

"I love petite sandwiches!" exclaimed Chloe. "It feels so… British." She scratched her head. "Does it seem odd to be serving afternoon tea and cucumber sandwiches in the capital of the United States?"

"Psst!" said Ofelia, covering her mouth. "Julia Jennings is in the middle of the room, near the center column."

"Okay, got it," mumbled Chloe, who was chewing on a mini gouda-filled croissant she had taken from a passing server. "So, what's the plan?"

"I need you to distract her so I can take her briefcase."

"I think I missed that. Can you repeat what you said because I'm not sure I understand?"

"I need you to distract her so I can take her briefcase."

"That's what I thought you said. Dang it."

"Ofelia, let me explain a couple of things to you, " said Chloe, her voice tinged with reluctance, as she chewed on a mini egg roll. "I'm not trained in espionage or being a decoy. And I'm also definitely not certifiably crazy."

Ofelia grabbed her hand and pulled her toward Julia, weaving around roving servers and isolated pairs of minglers. As they approached Julia, who was leading a discussion near a catering table with half dozen people, Ofelia silently slipped away into the crowd.

"Ofelia?" called Chloe, just feet away from Julia. "Oh, where has she gone to now?"

Julia stopped speaking and, turning toward Chloe, her grin widened as she registered who she was. Her coterie of like-minded, do-good associates, dressed in Ann Taylor dresses and blue blazers and slacks that did not belie their white-collar approach to humanitarian work, angled their heads in Chloe's direction inquiringly.

Ofelia was standing on the opposite side of the center column, her back pressed against it, her hand cupping her right ear to improve her hearing. Before heading to the National Press Club, she changed into a tan halter top with brown crop pants and brown block-heel sandals blending into the wooden center column. Or at least, she thought, the outfit helped her camouflage.

"Ah, Dr. Burgos!" proclaimed a wiry, elderly man with a gray beard, red beret, oversized suit and walking cane.

"Shhhh!" hissed Ofelia, waving the man away dismissively.

"Did you say something, doctor?" He tried again, louder this time. "I've been having issues with my hearing aids."

Ofelia stared at Joseph Duchamps, whom she had known for years. He was an expert in monitoring and evaluation but should have retired at least fifteen years earlier. His principal contribution to public health projects at this point was getting AARP discounts for car rentals.

"So nice to see you, Mr. Duchamps. But I can't speak right now. I'm practicing deep listening."

"Is that so? I'm not familiar with that. What are you listening to?"

"I am transcending the intrapersonal and interpersonal levels to focus deeply on the voices of the group. Good day to you!"

Ofelia shut her eyes and struck a meditative pose, praying that he would get the hint. A couple of minutes later, slowly opening one eye, then the other, she felt relieved. "Coast is clear!" she said under her breath.

She sidled her way toward Julia, her back still against the center column, until she was just a couple feet away from her. She could make out Chloe, who was blushing from embarrassment. Julia appeared to have just made the group laugh.

"There's nothing wrong with community college, mind you," said Julia. "It's certainly a more affordable option. But if I were USAID looking for experts in the field, I would caution that you get what you pay for."

This line is so old, thought Ofelia. *So what if Chloe has an associate's degree?* She scanned the floor and noticed that Julia had placed her briefcase a foot away from where Ofelia was standing. It was the same briefcase she had seen her carry when they met at the Ronald Reagan Building. It was a beige, Italian leather briefcase, with brown leather handles and a black fabric shoulder strap. It was stuffed with a laptop and papers and had not been zipped shut.

Bingo! she told herself. Ofelia did another quick survey of the room, then bent down and pulled the briefcase to her.

Shocking how disorganized she is! Ofelia thought, as she started rummaging through its contents. She found a presentation folder with the Chemonics logo and pulled it out. It was bulging with paper and had many handwritten notes and sticky pads.

What a bore! Academic papers.

She did a quick skim, then placed it back in the briefcase. She dug deeper into the bag and retrieved a small box. *Keto fat bombs? All natural chocolate bars with only ONE net carb,* she read. *If she wasn't such an insulting snoot, I'd ask her opinion about this!*

She returned the keto bars to the briefcase and pulled out a leather portfolio binder. She unzipped it and found several pens and a calculator tucked into pockets on one side. On the other side, there was a legal pad with handwritten, bulleted notes. It was difficult to decipher the cursive, but she could make out the words *RFP win plan* and *taking out the competition.* Attached to the lower right of the legal plan was a receipt from the Ritz-Carlton in Georgetown, Washington, DC.

"Ha!" Ofelia yelled out loud. "I knew it!"

The moment may have gotten the better of her, because she had intended to be more subtle with her detective work.

"What do you think you're doing!?"

Ofelia was still crouching over the briefcase, portfolio binder in both hands, looking up at Julia. "Well," she huffed, "that was what I was going to ask you!"

"That is *my* briefcase!" cried Julia, her eyes bulging.

"There you go! So you admit it!"

"What are you talking about? Give me back *my* briefcase!"

Ofelia closed the binder, placing it back in the briefcase, then stood up defensively, cradling the bag protectively like a quarterback. A hush fell over the lounge, and a crowd formed around Julia and Ofelia. Chloe was a few feet behind Julia, next to a server who had followed the commotion out of curiosity. She was chewing a brie-and-apricot sausage roll thoughtfully, her eyes glued to the women like a spectator at *Monday Night Football*.

"I will not," said Ofelia stubbornly. "I want to know what this all means!?"

"Have you lost your mind?"

"What were you doing at the Ritz last night?"

"I'm not having this conversation with you. You're a nutjob," said Julia, stepping forward and reaching for the briefcase.

Ofelia jumped left, sending Julia reeling to the floor. "You thought you could get away with it, huh? You're trying to sabotage your highly qualified competitor!"

Julia lay on the floor, her face crimson, glaring at Ofelia. The crowd was larger now and becoming more animated.

"I'm betting the chalk on the blonde," said someone in the crowd.

"What are the odds?" asked another.

"I'm taking the little brunette!"

Julia jumped to her feet and lunged again at Ofelia, grabbing the briefcase's dangling shoulder strap. Ofelia tried to swing out Julia's way, pirouetting toward Chloe, but Julia held on tightly and pulled her along.

"Mine!" cried Julia.

"No! Mine!" yelled Ofelia.

A vigorous tug of war ensued, with Ofelia pulling the briefcase in one direction and Julia pulling the shoulder strap in the other.

"You thought you were so clever, booking my room at the Ritz," panted Ofelia. "Thought I'd just sleep in and miss the orals!"

There was a ripping sound as the briefcase tore apart, causing Ofelia and Julia to plunge to the floor. The laptop crashed, and papers flew everywhere. Ofelia sprawled on her back, her limbs spread in an ungainly sight. She stared at the ceiling lights and observed, momentarily, that two of the light bulbs needed to be replaced.

What she remembered in the immediate aftermath of the fight was a blur. At least two muscular men in white polyester button-down shirts and navy blue clip-on ties lifted her by each arm. They carried her to the elevator and then outside, leaving her sitting on the street curb. It had begun to rain, and puddles were forming around her feet.

"Um, so that went reasonably well," said Chloe a few minutes later, crouching down beside Ofelia. "You know, it could have been, theoretically, worse."

Thirty minutes later, Ofelia and Chloe were sitting in the backseat of a cab, soaked and shivering. "I *suppose…*" said

Ofelia, sloshing in her seat. "I suppose I may have slightly jumped to conclusions."

"Could be."

"I mean, in retrospect, I might recall a bit of a conversation with Julia last night. Something about her sister's bachelorette party and having a night out on the town."

"Ah, yes. She mentioned that to the security guards. Among other four-letter words."

"She just seemed guilty."

"Yeah, she has a guilty look to her."

"So full of it."

The cab's brakes squealed, and the driver leaned his elbow into the horn. "Watch where you're going, you lousy, no good, good-for-nothing!" he shouted, as the rain whipped Ofelia in the face through the driver's open side window.

"I'm really at a loss about this whole situation," said Ofelia, hugging herself to keep warm.

"It's hard to understand," replied Chloe.

"It's the fair-weather drivers," interjected the driver. "They can't handle rain. And God forbid the snow..."

"Um..."

"You know, the worst thing about this city is how people are always trying to get ahead. Cutting corners, weaving in and out of lanes, being reckless and selfish. I mean, if this isn't the epitome of a rat race, then I don't know what is."

Ofelia stared at herself in the rearview mirror, noticing her wet and matted hair, stained top in several spots, smudged mascara and a strong resemblance to a very sorry-looking drowned rat.

"You didn't have to escort me back," said Ofelia to Chloe as she slogged through the Ritz Carlton's lobby toward her room moments later.

"What, and leave you stranded on the curb?" said Chloe, placing her arm on Ofelia's sopping shoulder. "We're friends.

Plus, I wanted to be around just in case you decided Kendrick wasn't your type."

Ofelia groaned. "I completely forgot about him. I should skip dinner..."

"Nuh uh, sista, you're not missing this. He's expecting you in an hour."

They stepped into the elevator, and Chloe began humming.

"He's so fine
Do-lang-do-lang-do-lang
Wish he were mine
Do-lang-do-lang-do-lang."

Ofelia's cell phone buzzed as they entered her hotel room. She had unread text messages.

(Mathew) *Everything okay?*

(Everly) *Heard about the incident.*

(Everly) *Don't worry. Go out and enjoy your last night in DC. Your keynote will be a smash tomorrow!*

(Luis) *Rough day?*

(Mother) *OFeliA. CALL me. What happened today.???*

(Mother) *you work TOo much*

(Mother) *STRESS makes you GAssy!!*

"Wonderful. Who doesn't know about today?"

"I didn't want to bring it up," said Chloe.

"Bring what up?"

"Well..." said Chloe, shuffling her feet nervously.

"Well?"

"You're trending on YouTube."

"I see."

"Half a million views already."

"Is that good?"

"Viral."

Ofelia's fastidiousness in packing extra outfits when she traveled paid off for once. She had just taken a shower and slipped on a high-notched collar, V-neck red dress with puffed shoulders and a belted waist. She felt much more herself now and had some time to think while soaking under the hot water after Chloe had left.

The messages, *You work too much* and *You'll be a smash,* rang through her head.

Shortly after 7:00 p.m., Kendrick was waiting for Ofelia in the lobby lounge bar in the same spot she had seen him earlier in the afternoon. He was still wearing his light gray pinstripe suit, but had ditched the tie, leaving his collar open. Boris was curled on his lap and began wagging his tail when he saw Ofelia approaching.

"Ofelia!" exclaimed Kendrick, placing Boris on the ground. "You look lovely tonight."

"Apologies for being late," she said, adjusting her glasses. "You don't happen to watch YouTube often, do you?"

"YouTube? Uh, sometimes, I guess. For the occasional cat video. Why do you ask?"

"Oh, no reason. Just making small talk," she said, grabbing Boris by the leash and hurriedly walking toward the door. "Where to?"

Kendrick jogged after her. "I made a reservation for Filomena's. It's not far."

Filomena's was crowded, but felt homey, if a little dated. It was a traditional Italian restaurant in the heart of Georgetown, with antique furniture, heavy oak tables and Murano-glass chandeliers. They took a seat in the back, where Boris could sit under the table without causing any distractions.

"Do you eat here much?" asked Ofelia, twiddling her thumbs nervously. She had not been on a date in over a year, *although this is most certainly not a* proper *date*, she thought.

Kendrick placed his hand on hers reassuringly and smiled. "I just want to say again how stunning you look tonight. Your hair is beautifully coiffed."

Ofelia felt her face reddening and pulled her hand back. She had been perfecting the art of coiffing.

"My mother's side is Italian," continued Kendrick. "I've always been drawn to these types of restaurants. Reminds me of my grandmother, Nonna Giuseppina."

A waitress walked over and handed them two menus.

"Could you bring some Gaudianello sparkling water and a bottle of Produttori del Barbaresco?" asked Kendrick as he took off his suit jacket and placed it on the back of his chair.

"When I first saw you," he said to Ofelia, "I felt we had some sort of connection. I would never have asked a stranger to watch my little Boris, but with you it was different."

"Well, that's nice. Too bad I don't remember our conversation."

"You have an amazing life story. What you've accomplished. Being so well respected in your industry."

Ofelia sat a little more upright at that statement. *I would never mention how well respected I was to anyone. That would be, well, pompous like Julia.*

"The conference event page has a nice profile on you," said Kendrick. "Would you like to walk me through your keynote speech?"

Ofelia relaxed and sat back in her chair. Glancing to her right, she saw a couple, their arms extended across the table, their hands intertwined.

"It may come as a surprise, but I'm not a fan of public speaking. Maybe it's because English isn't my first language."

Kenrick nodded empathetically. "A lot of health professionals struggle with public speaking."

"It's like I have a stodgy file clerk in my brain who decides to slam the file cabinet shut to my hippocampus when I have to give presentations to large groups of people. It's very annoying."

The server walked over to their table and served the wine and sparkling water.

Kendrick stared momentarily at his wine glass, then clapped his hands excitedly. "I have a thought. Have you heard of the power pose?"

"Can't say that I have."

"Okay. So, there's a psychologist who gave a Ted Talk a few years ago about how our body language affects not only how people think of us, but how we think of ourselves. If you take a private moment in front of the mirror and hold your arms up like this," said Kendrick, raising his arms up in a V-shape to demonstrate, "it will make you feel more confident before a speech. Why don't you give it a try in the restroom, then come back and practice your speech on me?"

Ofelia drummed her fingers on the table and stared at the couple again. They appeared to be in their mid-twenties. The woman wore a sleeveless, pink summer dress and was small and fragile next to what Ofelia assumed was her boyfriend.

"You know what? Why not?" she said, standing up and straightening her dress. "I'll be back shortly."

Ofelia made her way through the crowded dining area to the restroom. As she started pushing the restroom door open, she turned back, momentarily, and glimpsed at Kendrick leaning on the table. He dropped something into her wine glass.

Of course, she thought. *What a shame.*

Ofelia whirled around and swung the restroom door open, stepping in front of the wall-mounted mirror. She brushed the hair from her eyes and examined herself. She looked sharp and was feeling more confident already, certain of what she needed to do. She spread her feet wide apart, shut her eyes and inhaled deeply. Everything was coming into focus. Her mind was quieter. She slowly raised her arms up in a V-shape and breathed.

"You're fired, you impertinent file clerk!" she shouted, opening her eyes. To her left, a couple feet away, stood the woman in the pink dress. Ofelia smiled. "Care to join me?" The woman nodded shyly, then closed her eyes and raised her arms slowly in the air. "Fake it till you make it!" she shouted.

"There you go. Let it all out," said Ofelia. "Although I prefer, practice till you perfect it."

"My boyfriend's a royal ass," said the woman. "I caught him cheating on me last week, and now he's trying to make it up to me."

A toilet flushed, and a woman exited the stall. She washed her hands, then stood to the right of Ofelia. "Oh no, that won't do, honey," said the woman, raising her arms in the air. "Dump him. You have that power."

"My date's trying to drug me," said Ofelia matter-of-factly.

"What! Oh my God! That's horrible," said the woman in the pink dress.

"What a bastard!" said the other woman.

"It's a shame. He is very handsome," said Ofelia. "And sadly, I think he was on it last night as well."

A waitress entered the bathroom and stood next to the woman in the pink dress. "Power pose!" she exclaimed, lifting her arms in the air. "I have the most asinine customer. He is so incredibly rude."

"It all makes sense now," said Ofelia. "My cab driver summed it up perfectly. There are certain people in this city who feel like they can cut corners to make it, no matter the trouble that might cause others."

"Well, no one is putting us down tonight," said the waitress. "Enough is enough!"

When Ofelia returned to her table and sat down. Kendrick smiled and placed his cell phone on the table. He had been texting with someone. Nearby, the woman in the pink dress sat primly on the edge of her seat and glanced at Ofelia.

"How do you feel?" asked Kenrick.

"I have to hand it to you, I feel amazing," she said, staring directly at him. "Much surer of myself."

As if on cue, the woman in the pink dress tossed her water in her boyfriend's face. There was an audible gasp in the room as she stood up, spreading her feet apart with her hands on her hips in a Wonder Woman pose, and said calmy but forcefully, "We're through! You're a cheat, and you can't buy back my trust."

Kendrick, distracted by the commotion, didn't see Ofelia switch their wine glasses. The woman in the pink dress turned to Ofelia, smiled, then strode out of the restaurant to scattered applause. "Wow! Let's drink to that," said Ofelia, raising her wine glass to her mouth and taking a sip.

Kendrick, still unsettled from the commotion, raised his glass, and took a deep gulp.

"That was something," said Kendrick, eyeing the wet man at the nearby table. He took another large swig of wine and shook his head. "But do I love Produttori del Barbaresco. Can you taste hints of black cherry and truffle?"

"It's a complex affair," said Ofelia, raising her wine glass again. "And here's another toast to making connections."

Kendrick raised his glass, took another gulp of wine, and sat back comfortably in his chair. "To making connections," he replied. "Now, how about that speech?"

"Good evening," interjected the server Ofelia had seen in the restroom earlier. "I'll be taking your orders."

"Wonderful. How about the most special item on your menu?" Ofelia looked at Kendrick imploringly. "After all, you *are* a surgeon, and I'm sure you don't mind splurging a little, since I watched little Boris here."

Ofelia thought she saw Kendrick flinch.

"I'll take the Linguini Cardinale with lobster," said Ofelia, skimming the menu, searching for the most expensive bottle of wine. "And a bottle of 2016 Masseto," she added. *Priced at $1,195. Ha!*

"So, about my speech," said Ofelia after Kenrick had placed his order. " I doubt you'll remember a word of it. And by the time our food comes around, I don't think you'll be a tremendous help with the dry run."

Kendrick looked puzzled. "I'm sorry. Did I miss something?"

"I never heard Everly speak about you specifically," Ofelia continued. "I knew she came from a large Catholic family. But then I thought about how odd it was that a surgeon was attending an international health policy conference. Plausible, but unlikely. This conference attracts NGOs and government types," She took another sip of wine. "This is splendid, I must admit. Anyway, I decided to look you up on LinkedIn. I thought, let me search for Kendrick O'Brien and see what comes up. Lo and behold, there you were… dressed in this same pinstripe suit you're wearing now. Your occupation: Mid-Atlantic sales representative for Industrial Boilers."

"There's obviously a misunderstanding," said Kendrick uncomfortably, adjusting his shirt collar. "O'Brien is a common name."

"Sure, O'Brien is relatively common. But Kendrick O'Brien from Reston, Virginia, isn't. Plus, I found photos of you and Everly on Facebook. Speaking of Everly... She's ambitious, overly ambitious, and has been vying for a promotion the past couple of years. I'm all about promotions, but not at the expense of someone else. Not by cutting corners or sabotage. That was her plan. Drop a couple of roofies in my drink while I'm dining at 1789, then have her brother, for some reason I can't fully explain, check me into my hotel room. Hoping that I don't show up to my presentation or, at the bare minimum, making me woozy enough that I bomb it. And it was a good ruse. Staying at a luxury hotel was a nice touch, and very distracting. Her dog was also adorable, and. she knew that I'm a sucker for puppies, even odd-looking puppies that desperately need grooming and braces." She reached under the table and rubbed Boris's head. "No offense, Boris, you're a sweetheart."

Kendrick rubbed his eyes. He was struggling to express outrage while mounting a counter-defense. Ofelia watched as beads of sweat formed on his forehead. His eyelids were drooping, and his head was swaying.

"Nawhhaa, looooksss here," he slurred before slumping in his seat.

Ofelia took another sip of her wine and stood up. She walked around the table and stood behind Kenrick.

"Kendrick, you appear to be sleepy," she said, reaching into his suit's flap pocket and pulled a bottle of Rohypnol. "Found it!" she exclaimed.

The waitress brought their dinners to the table. "He doesn't seem to be up to eating his antipasti," she said.

"I don't think he is," Ofelia said, showing her the bottle. "I think he may have overdone it."

"Do you want me to call the police?" whispered the server in Ofelia's ear.

"No. I don't think that will be necessary," Ofelia said.

Ofelia grabbed his cell phone and swiped it on, using his face to log in.

"What do you see?" the waitress asked curiously.

"Text messages from his sister. She is a coworker of mine."

"No way!"

Ofelia took a screenshot of the text messages and sent them to her cell phone number.

"This message is interesting," said Ofelia to the waitress, who leaned in to take a closer look. "Kendrick," read Ofelia out loud, "don't skimp on the pills. We need her out cold, and then this promotion is mine. We can finally move out of this awful apartment."

"Wow. That's low."

"I think it's time I called a cab."

The ride to Everly's apartment took longer than it should have, because Ofelia had the driver pick up Chloe along the way. Kenrick was snoring in the passenger seat, and Ofelia and Chloe were sitting in the rear. It was dark and drizzling outside, but Ofelia felt more alert than she had in days.

"I have to admit, Ofelia," said Chloe after some time, "I find it hard to fathom why Everly would go to such lengths to sabotage you. I mean, it's just bonkers.

"I don't know. Clearly, she wanted a promotion. I would have thought that there were easier ways to go about getting one"

"She did, to her credit, I suppose, put you up in a nice hotel."

"I'm not complaining about that," said Ofelia, stroking Boris' back. But she wanted me out of the way. All the big-wigs from RTI are going to be at the conference tomorrow."

"You know, she may have lost us the contract because of her shenanigans."

Everly lived on the first floor of a three-story, brown brick apartment complex that was built in the 1970s and was close to Leesburg Pike. The building was unattractive, and although Ofelia could see why Everly would want to move, it was in a quiet, safe neighborhood that was certainly nicer than the crowded three-flat she'd spent her childhood in.

I guess everything is a matter of perspective, she thought. *We all want different things, but what matters most is how you go about getting what you want.*

Ofelia stepped out of the cab, parked in front of Everly's unit, and walked to the driver's side window."I'll pay you double if you help us deliver this gentleman to his apartment." *Technically, Kendrick will double your fare, but who's asking?* She thought.

The driver exited the car like a torpedo. It was impressive since he was a rotund individual. "Okay, so I'll lift him out of his seat, and then you'll get under each arm," he said, running around the car, then opening the passenger-side door. He did a few squats as warms ups before reaching in. "And here we go, one, two…"

Kendrick dropped out of the car onto his bottom, into a large puddle. His head slumped over his chest, his hands dangled from his side, and he continued to snore.

"Gosh dang it," said the driver. "He slipped right outta my hands. He's like a pile of lead."

"He looks peaceful," said Chloe. "Should we just leave him here?"

Ofelia looked at Kendrick. He did look peaceful.

"Nah. He might catch something. Who knows what's crawling around the ground?"

"I'll grab him by his feet," said the driver. "You ladies grab him from under each arm. Okay?"

They lifted him this time. There was a tearing sound as they picked him up.

"Oh dear, I think we've torn his pants," said Chloe, panting.

"It'll help with ventilation," huffed Ofelia. "He's sopping wet."

They shuffled their way slowly to the front entrance, then placed him upright against the wall near Everly's apartment.

"Let me run and get Boris," said Chloe.

Ofelia rang the doorbell to Everly's apartment. The cab driver lit a cigarette and walked a few feet away. After a minute or so, the door slowly creaked open. A woman in a nightgown peered out of the partially opened door, then unlatched the chain lock.

"Ofelia," she asked, bewildered. "Is that you?"

"Hi, Everly. Yes, it is. *Surprise!*" said Ofelia, grinning. "Oh, and I've also brought along Kendrick." She pointed to the unconscious figure slumped against the wall. "He's a little lethargic right now. Took a few too many sleepy pills."

Everly's face went white. She placed her hand in front of her mouth.

"I think the pills were meant for me," continued Ofelia, pulling out her cell phone and showing it to Everly. "Based on your text messages to Kendrick this evening, you didn't want to *skimp* on the pills. Much stronger dose than the ones you gave me on Sunday night."

There was a high-pitched bark as Boris sprinted past the cab driver and Ofelia, spinning excitedly in circles in front of Everly.

"Boris," whimpered Everly quietly.

"Good ol' Boris," said Ofelia. "We got along well. Oh, and let me introduce you to our cab driver..."

"Ajani," he interjected. "Nice to meet you. Fascinating drama, I must add."

"And here's Chloe!"

Chloe was filming the entire episode on her cell phone. "Good evening, Everly. We hope we didn't disturb you, but we needed to make a delivery," she said.

A thud echoed as a small cloud of dust drifted into the air. Everly lay passed out, face down in the doorway, with Ofelia, Ajani and Chloe standing over her.

"Ouch," said Chloe, placing her phone back in her purse.

"We didn't even need to give her the sleepy pills," said Ofelia.

"Doesn't look like she broke anything," said Ajani, poking his index finger at her repeatedly.

"I think this is a fitting ending to our evening, don't you?" asked Ofelia. "Let's bring them inside and wish them adieu."

The main ballroom at the National Press Club was packed. Several hundred attendees for the International Conference on Public Health were sitting theater-style around the main stage. It was just after 9:00 a.m. and the host was making his way to the podium.

The sun had come out and was shining through the sliding glass doors on each side of the main stage. Ofelia was seated in a chair facing the audience, in front of the curtains closest to the stage. She could make out Chloe and Mathew, seated a few rows back, as well as Ms. Henderson, the USAID contracting officer in the front row.

Well, I guess this is it, she thought. *I'm really doing this.* Ofelia placed her hands on her lap and narrowed her eyes.

I am a powerful woman! She said to herself, spreading her feet apart to make herself feel bigger. She had never found the speaker notes she had so painstakingly prepared. She figured Everly or Kendrick had taken them, but regardless, she concluded they had done her a favor. She didn't need them. Today, the file clerk in her brain was not going to dictate the terms of her speech.

"Welcome to the National Press Club, the world's leading professional organization for journalists..." began the host.

She felt a little sorry for Everly. After all, she had to report the incident to Human Resources, and it was certainly not the sort of incident any responsible company could ignore. She assumed she wouldn't see Everly around the office much from now on.

While Everly wasn't old enough to have a mid-life crisis, there was no doubt, in Ofelia's mind, that Everly was having a quarter-life crisis. While she could relate to Evelyn's desperation and lack of confidence, she couldn't relate to the drugging part—that was crazy to her.

It's hard to explain, she thought, *why we have our discontents. We're so privileged here. And yet even successful people, such as Everly and myself, seem to hit inexplicable U-curves in life. We become consumed with what we'd lack and lose sight of just how lucky many of us are. Here I am, a first-*

generation woman from the inner city, delivering a keynote address to hundreds of public health professionals!

I suppose I should apologize to Julia. Ofelia sighed. *She's such a high-brow, stiff-necked elitist, but she's working in a field trying to help young women and mothers all over the world, just like me. So, I'll just tip my hat to her and tell her I'm sorry.*

"And now, without further ado, let's bring to the stage our keynote speaker, Dr. Ofelia Burgos!" exclaimed the host.

Ofelia rose to her feet, She could feel the sun on her back. She closed her eyes, inhaled deeply and lifted her chest and head toward the ceiling while stretching out her arms. She could feel the energy flowing in and around her and knew that everything she needed to say, everything she was all about, was fully visible. Nothing could hold her back this morning.

If she had been paying attention, she would have noticed that Ms. Henderson, a woman with a perpetual frown, was the first to stand up, raising her arms in the air with a slight but perceptible smile. Chloe, Mathew and every man and woman in the audience followed. And when Ofelia finally opened her eyes and stepped onto the stage, she saw a sea of people reaching to the sky, unencumbered by meddlesome file clerks and inner demons. Despite her small stature, she had never felt more significant and powerful than she did on that stage.

BOO

Bobby "Boo" Buchowski had a bazooka for an arm. He had one of the most explosive fastballs in baseball, clocking in at 105 miles an hour. His fastball was so intimidating and unpredictable that opposing hitters would go to great lengths to avoid him. "Skipper, I strained my calf," was a common refrain. Or "I ate something bad." The more religious types might say, "My nephew has a bar mitzvah" or "It's my sister's *quinceañera*."

The antics earned Bobby the nickname Boo because his pitching scared the hell out of just about everyone. The issue wasn't so much the velocity, but his lack of control. There were several sad instances of batters being lifted unconscious onto a gurney after being struck by his pitch. To exacerbate matters, these scenes were replayed on SportsCenter, a popular news sports program, solely for ratings.

However, his most devastating pitch was not his fastball, but his slowball, otherwise known as the eephus pitch, the super-changeup, the balloon ball, the off-off-speed pitch, the gondola or parachute. The coaching staff referred to it as Pitch Number Two, since Boo had only two types of pitches in his repertoire.

The problem with Pitch Number Two was that it slowed the game down. Baseball is a game requiring patience, especially for a spectator of minor league action, but there comes a time when it's in everyone's interest to get the game over with. Boo threw Pitch Number Two most of the time, and since it clocked in a hair over 45 miles per hour after a lengthy windup, his mound appearances drew vociferous groans from the stands.

It was Boo's unique approach to the game that relegated him to the Charlotte Knights in Triple-A. This was certainly an achievement, given that Triple-A is the closest to the majors and is full of talented players, including those with extensive major league experience. But for those who knew Boo well, especially his assistant pitching coach Kenny Kirk, he was a disappointment. An underachiever.

"He just can't put it all together," Kirk would say.

After the 2001 season and Boo's lackluster earned run average of 6.00 as a starting pitcher, the coaching staff moved him into a middle reliever role for the 2002 season. Nick "Cappy" Capra, the general manager, figured that Boo's advanced age—he was 34 years old—was causing him to lose steam and throw erratically after going for three or more innings. Cappy was desperate for pitchers since the Charlotte Knights had lost several of them to free agency, and he still believed Boo could contribute.

Kirk was more skeptical. He wanted to see how Boo performed in Spring training. If Boo couldn't pull it off working with Carlos Burgos, a veteran catcher recently acquired from the Rockies, then Kirk was done with him.

Carlos wasn't aware of Boo's predicament when he arrived in Phoenix for spring training. Players moved around the leagues constantly, sometimes falling out of favor with the coaching staff and getting demoted or cut. All he knew was that he was going to handle Boo and help mentor some of the younger players.

When Carlos stepped onto the field one early Monday morning in February for the first workout of Spring training, he wondered if baseball life was worth it. He had been recovering from an oblique muscle strain at his parent's house in Humboldt Park and had been wearing an uncomfortable compression bandage during his stay. He knew he was one awkward throw away from involuntary retirement, and he found this reality unsettling. And the coaching staff weren't exactly rolling out the welcome mat, either. This was the time of year when he had to compete for his job all over again. Even though his batting average was up, and he had certain verbal assurances, he knew he was constantly auditioning.

"Good morning, cream puffs," said Rob Bowers, the field coordinator, addressing the players assembled around the pitcher's mound. "Hope you got your beauty rest."

Can't say that I did, thought Carlos ruefully.

"As you can see," continued Coach Bowers, "this year we've brought on more players than we have roster spots for. Y'all know what this means. So do your best if you want to be with us tomorrow."

Carlos glanced at the players. There were more than twenty-five pitchers and catchers on the field. He didn't know most of them, but he recognized Jorge "Jecito" López, a relief pitcher he had played with a few years ago with the Colorado Springs Sky Sox. Jorge was tall, barrel-chested and wore a Figaro gold chain with a crucifix pendant and had a tattoo of the Virgin Mary on his forearm. He had a nervous twitch and made the sign of the cross before each pitch.

Next to Jecito stood Sonny DeMarco, a neatly groomed starter sporting a pencil mustache that gave him a dastardly, brooding look that always endeared him to a female fan base.

Carlos had played with Sonny when he was called up to play Single-A ten years earlier. He had witnessed him exchange "autographs" with women who otherwise didn't seem to have much interest in the game.

The only other player he knew was Boo. He had seen his odd eephus pitch up close, having attempted to hit the high-arching ball in more than one game. Boo had a way of slightly varying the speed and causing it to drop and move in unpredictable ways. When Boo was in the zone, with his deceptive arm speed and the wild movement of the ball, he could strike out the side with the eephus alone. When he added his fastball to the mix, he could be unhittable.

Carlos had also observed Boo on off nights, when at first, he seemed like an ace but then fell apart in the late innings. That was when the opposing team's hits and runs piled up and the coaches pulled him from the game.

Boo had a foul temper, and the wildness of his pitches spread his distemper like a virus. His bright blue eyes radiated with a turbulent ultramarine intensity that shone from his kelp-like mane and black, bushy beard. He stood taller than Jecito, and while he wasn't the tallest player on the field, he was built like a fire truck.

"I want you to get through to him," Cappy had said to Carlos over the phone when they first traded for him to Charlotte.

Carlos hadn't thought about that comment much, but looking at Boo, who was on the other side of the infield from him, it made sense now. Boo was a frown wrapped in a machine gun. Carlos would need to give constructive feedback with extreme care.

"All right, ladies," Coach Bowers announced, "let's get the blood flowing with laps around the field."

As the players hurried to the sideline, there was distinct grumbling, their pace somewhere between speed-walking and a jog.

Carlos felt someone brush his shoulder and saw, to his right, a short, beer-bellied, sunburnt man in a sleeveless tank top, camouflage cargo shorts and Coors trucker hat. "Youse Carlos?" he asked, already working up a sweat.

"Yeah, that's Carlos," said Jecito, from Carlos' left. "They brought him here to handle Boo."

"Ahh, good. Boo's part of the Mad Dawgz now."

"The what?" said Carlos.

"The Mad Dawgz is our crew," said Jecito.

"Yeppers. He sure is a killa, but we're all skittish. Put Frankie in an ambewlance last year."

Carlos scratched the back of his neck. *Am I missing something?*

"I'm Big Mac, by the way," the sunburnt guy said, huffing as they made their way toward the outfield.

"Big Mac? Like the hamburger?" asked Carlos.

"Yeppers. Because of my big, burly physique."

Carlos glanced at Big Mac. There was no muscle definition anywhere on his body.

"I've been here for a spell. A founding member of the Mad Dawgz, as a matter of fact."

"Our bullpen's got some talent, man," said Jecito proudly.

Carlos had seen some film from the 2001 season, and talent wasn't the first word that came to mind.

"Boo's gonna take it up a level, if you can work your magic on him." Jecito added.

"Work my magic?" said Carlos.

"We heered 'bout your talents. They says youse a pitcher's whisperer."

Carlos wasn't sure what a pitcher's whisperer was, but he had no trouble managing games. He'd been around too long, and the game didn't rattle him the way it did some players.

"Well, I still have to make the cut," said Carlos. "You never know."

"Nah, youse shore a lock."

"I appreciate that," said Carlos. "What do you know about Boo?"

"Boo's ill. Gotta be careful."

"Is he contagious or something?"

"Nah, man," said Jecito. "Let me translate Big Mac for you. He hails from West, by God, Virginia."

"Barned in a double-wide, in a mountain holler, s'matter of fact."

"Boo got a bad temper. That's what he means. Boo is crazy, if you ask me."

"Don't believe those West Virginia jokes. You know marrying your first cousin is legal in New York?"

"I think Boo feels trapped here," continued Jecito. "He probably thinks he should be in the majors. Too late for him now."

"What's really crazy dat people just think of hillbillies in Appalatchua. I heard Puerto Ricans git hillbillies called *hebarrow*. They play Spanish bluegrass and all."

"They're called *jíbaros*, and Carlos *is* Puerto Rican. As I was saying, we're all counting on you this year. If you can make Boo right again, then we have a chance."

"Stop gossiping, ladies, and speed it up!" shouted Coach Bowers. "Three more laps!"

"Aw, come now! I got a crick in my backside from all this runnin'!"

Later that afternoon, Carlos was squatting in full gear behind home plate, waiting for Big Mac to deliver his pitch.

Coach Bowers had split the squad up into small groups to practice pitching accuracy. Four cones had been arranged in between home plate and the vicinity of the mound, with the first cone placed halfway to the mound, the second placed three-fourths of the way to the mound, the third placed at the mound and the fourth a quarter-distance beyond the mound. The idea was for each pitcher to show that they could throw strikes. Big Mac had thrown two balls and ten strikes from the first and second cones and was working on throwing strikes from the third cone now. He was up to seven strikes and two balls.

Big Mac was sweating heavily as he stared at Carlos. He began his pitching motion, his stride foot stepping forward as he released his fastball. It flew toward home base with good velocity, then dropped suddenly, bouncing in the dirt in front of Carlos, forcing him to block the ball with his chest.

"Focus, now!" shouted Coach Kirk from the sidelines.

"Let's go," encouraged Jecito.

"First day, Big Mac. We're all rusty," said Sean Lofter, another member of the Mad Dawgz.

"Clap up, you'ns! I got this," barked Big Mac. "This ain't no chore!"

Boo let out a loud guffaw at the remark and placed his thumbs in his jogger pants pockets.

Carlos glanced at Boo. It was the first thing he had heard from him all day.

"Easy does it," said Carlos reassuringly, returning his attention to Big Mac. "Hold on a sec."

Carlos stood up and trotted over to the mound.

"Look, Big Mac," whispered Carlos, "everything we do is a test. I don't want to get cut, and neither do you. You're a good pitcher, but I can tell you're rushing things."

"I believe you're right."

"It's not like you're missing the strike zone by a lot, but you need to slow down and visualize the ball coming off your fingertips, spinning in the air, breaking when and where you want it to break until it crosses home plate. You should feel the pitch from your toes to your forehead. You should feel good about what you're throwing because it all starts with your head. You're deciding what to do, and don't ever let the ball or the hitter dictate otherwise. You should feel positive about your pitches because you feel positive about yourself. You're Big Mac, and everything that you do, everything you say, has style and purpose."

Big Mac stared at Carlos with his mouth open.

"Come on, now," shouted Coach Kirk. "Let's get a move on."

Carlos returned to the plate and moved into his receiving crouch. He pounded his fist into his glove and locked eyes with Big Mac. They nodded in unison.

Big Mac threw a strike. Carlos nodded and tossed the ball back. Big Mac threw another strike. And another, all down the middle.

Coach Kirk scribbled into his notepad. "All right," he said, squinting at Carlos. "Not bad. Up next, Jecito."

Jecito sprinted to the first cone, high-fiving Big Mac as they switched places. He pointed his index finger at Carlos and then pointed at the sky, nodding his head vigorously as he began an animated dialogue with himself. Carlos raised an eyebrow as he waited for Jecito's conversation to end. He could see Jecito moving his lips. It was like there were two people out there. At one moment he would say something to himself and shake his head angrily from side to side; the next moment he would say something and hop up and down with excitement.

After a couple minutes of this, Jecito finally stood still, holding the ball in his pitching hand while staring determinedly at Carlos' glove. He took a small step forward, made the sign of the cross, then leaned backwards and lifted his right leg slightly as he cocked his arm and shifted his weight forward to deliver the fastball down the middle.

Okay. I guess he's going to throw full speed even from the first cone, thought Carlos.

Carlos tossed the ball back to Jecito, who repeated his stretch delivery motion. Another strike down the middle, full speed. Soon, Jecito had cleared the first cone with all strikes.

At the second cone, Jecito threw another eight strikes in a row before missing the strike zone for the first time on his ninth pitch. This caused him to curse, then apologize quickly to the Virgin Mary. "No offense meant, Blessed Mother!" he said out loud.

"Every time he misses, he gits plumb flustrated," chuckled Big Mac, elbowing Boo in the shoulder.

Boo slowly turned his head and side-eyed Big Mac.

Big Mac grinned sheepishly and rubbed his armpit. "Here he goes agin," he said hurriedly, pointing at Jecito as he began his pitching motion.

Jecito cleared the second cone and began to pitch from the third. He made five strikes in a row, then threw a wild pitch that got by Carlos and went to the backstop. "*¡Madre María!*" he cried, pacing back and forth on the mound while Carlos retrieved the ball.

Carlos jogged up to the mound with the ball in his hand. He had seen pitchers like Jecito in other clubs. "Jecito, what are you doing throwing heat like that?"

Jecito dropped his head and shuffled his feet on the ground. He looked winded. "I want to show my best stuff."

"Well, it's not working. You're overdoing it," said Carlos, pushing Jecito's chin up with his glove, so they were looking eye to eye. "Throw at seventy percent speed, *mi bróder*. There's only so many pitches an arm can take before it breaks down. Take a deep breath and shake your arms and shoulders to stay loose before you start your delivery. I think it will help."

Jecito nodded. Carlos slapped Jecito on his posterior with his glove, an antic that would be called harassment in most other professions. Jecito wiped away a tear.

"He called me *a brother,*" he said, as Carlos ran back to home plate.

Jecito exhaled and shook his shoulders and arms. Carlos thought he already looked more relaxed. Jecito made the sign of the cross and began his delivery motion, releasing the ball with greater precision now. Carlos watched it cross the center of the plate and smiled.

"It's just you and the mitt," said Carlos as he tossed the ball back to Jecito.

Jecito caught the ball and paced back and forth briefly, shaking his shoulders and arms to stay loose. He threw another strike. Then another.

When Jecito finished his drill, which ended shortly after Carlos' pep talk, Boo walked up to the mound. There was no high-fiving, no words of encouragement, no nod of solidarity. Carlos could tell that Boo didn't want to be there, that he resented being in the bullpen.

"Here comes Big Bad Boo," said Carlos under his breath. "Let's see what you got."

"As a reminder, you're pitching from the stretch," Coach Kirk shouted.

Boo squinted at Carlos and placed his pivot foot next to the first cone. He appeared calm and balanced. Carlos could see him rubbing the seams on the ball with his fingers.

Boo spat and began his delivery. He lifted his lead knee toward his pivot leg, swinging his pitching arm back while his gloved hand extended in front of him. Carlos couldn't tell if he was going to throw a fastball and braced for impact. Boo lifted his pitching hand into the air as he shifted his momentum forward and released the ball. It was an off-speed pitch, arcing high in the air like a Bugs Bunny curveball.

"Strike!" cried Big Mac.

"Seen nothing like it, *hombre*," said Jecito encouragingly.

Boo grunted and caught the ball from Carlos. He repeated his setup and threw the same pitch for another strike. Soon he had cleared the first and second cones, with no balls.

Carlos stood up as Boo moved to the third cone at the pitching mound.

"Okay, Boo," he said, "let's mix it up a bit. Show me something different."

Boo nodded and moved into his pitching stance on the mound. Coach Kirk stepped behind Carlos to inspect Boo's pitching mechanics.

Boo spat and began his delivery. *If this is his fastball,* thought Carlos, *then good, his delivery is consistent.*

Boo lifted his lead leg in the air and repeated the same cocking motion as he launched the ball. There was no arcing change-up this time. Carlos thought of the time when, as a kid, he had made CO_2 cartridge-powered wooden race cars with his brother. They would race them on the smooth floors of the hallway in their three-flat. He could recall the steam shooting from the cartridge as the cars rocketed across the floor. That was the image that came to mind when Boo delivered his fastball.

Unfortunately for Coach Kirk, the only thing to pop into his head at that moment was Boo's erratic fastball, which ricocheted off his forehead, knocking his cap off his head and dropping him to the ground like a sack of potatoes.

"Oh boy!" cried Jecito.

"Holy crap!" shouted Sean.

"Ah... I reckon he just killed our coach! Git him to the horespital!"

A few weeks later, Carlos was sitting in an armchair in his bedroom at the Comfort Inn and Suites with his parents on speakerphone. It was a Monday night, and the team was getting ready to play the first games of spring training the upcoming weekend.

"*Nene*, we are so excited to see you this weekend," said Carlos' mother, Josephina.

"We're proud of you," said his father, Roberto. "You're a baseball star. Living the high life."

Carlos glanced over at Big Mac, his roommate the past week, who was walking from the living room to the bedroom wearing nothing but a white Hanes sports brief, partially obscured by his pasty beer belly. Minor league clubs typically had their players room together as a cost savings measure.

"Yeah, right, living the high life," said Carlos. "I'm excited to see you too, but it's a long trip and you really don't need to come down."

"We always make it to your first games. It's a Burgos tradition," said his father.

Carlos thought about this tradition. Last year, his parents got into a debate with a Dominican couple about *pasteles*, arguing vigorously about the merits of the Puerto Rican version until they were escorted out of the stadium. The year before, his father knocked a hot dog vendor into the dugout, causing him to land headfirst in a trash bin. His father said it was an accident, but Carlos suspected sticker shock was a contributing factor.

"I know, Papi. But I'm with a new club. It might be better to wait and see if we're actually worth rooting for."

"Nonsense," said Carlos' father, "all the more reason to show our support now."

"And Luis is coming too," said his mother.

Carlos thought about his eldest brother, Luis, and his mood brightened. Luis was his idol growing up. He was the one who had gotten Carlos into baseball.

"And Javier and Chucho too," she added.

Carlos frowned. Javier, his cousin, and Javier's boyhood friend Chucho tended to get rowdy at games. He recalled the time Javier and Chucho's nonstop color commentary from the stands caused Carlos to pass a ball between his legs, causing the runner on first to steal second base.

"So, who, exactly, *isn't* coming this weekend?" cried Carlos.

"This will be a wonderful opportunity to spend time together as a family," his mother said enthusiastically.

Carlos sighed and stared at the cheap orange carpet. *Where did things go wrong?* he asked himself.

"Well, if you insist on coming, then you should try to make the most of it," he said, resigned that there was no stopping this. "You can do some tourist stuff… visit old Tucson or something."

"We booked our rooms at the Comfort Inn and Suites," his father said. "We wanted to stay close by, to be together."

"Of course you did," said Carlos, placing his face in his hand. "Of course, you did."

Coach Capra wasn't disposed to pre-game pep talks during spring training, but he gave one or two from time to time to reiterate his priorities for the club. Carlos was standing next to Big Mac and Jecito in a team huddle around the coach. Coach Kirk was standing next to Coach Capra, wearing a Charlotte Knights blue satin jacket.

"Yesterday the Bulls got the better of us," Capra began, addressing the Knights players in the center of the locker room. "We won't win all our games. It's Spring training and we have a long way to go. All I ask of you today is to focus." He slapped Coach Kirk on the shoulder for emphasis. "Focus on each play," he said, slapping Coach Kirk again.

"Focus on each pitch." Another slap. "Focus on each swing of the bat." A harder slap. "Stay focused on execution." More of a punch. "You know the fundamentals, but you can do a better job of executing them." A harder punch.

"Yeah, Coach," said one player.

"Sure, Skipper," said another.

"Mhmhfff," muttered Coach Kirk.

"They've got some talent. Andy Sheets, Emil Brown.... This young kid, Carl Crawford, he's a handful," continued Coach Capra, shaking Coach Kirk by the shoulder to emphasize his point. "Just remember that everything on the field counts. The small things, the small plays executed well add up, give us confidence as a team, help us connect as players and coaches. All right? Let's go get 'em, boys," concluded Capra, clapping his hands motivationally.

"Mhmhfff," came a whimper.

"Can't wait to git into the game," Big Mac said as the team began dispersing from the locker room.

"Yeah, man," said Jecito, who was rolling worry beads in one hand, creating a slight clicking noise. "Time to show Coach what we got."

"Soooo Carlos…youse git the start, two days in row," Big Mac said.

Carlos grabbed the helmet and chest protector from his locker and glanced at Big Mac. "I played okay yesterday, but I can do better," he replied.

"Man, you played solid," said Jecito. "You had a double and two singles."

"Youse hit that fastball smack-dab into right field. Youse ruint Carter's fifth inning."

Carlos smiled. *It felt good to perform so well on my first full start*, he thought. "Like coach said, we just need to execute better as a team," he said. "We got in a hole early. Otherwise, I think we would've had a chance."

"Yippers. We git to exicoot," said Big Mac as they made their way toward the field. "Oh, and youse reminds me, I seed your momma in the stands a little while ago."

Carlos stopped in his tracks. He started feeling clammy. "How do you know she was my mother?"

"Well, she was holding up a big sign that says 'Go Carlos, my little *luchador*. XXXOOO love Mami and Papi!' I think she war with some other folkses too."

"I see."

"My folks never come see me play," said Big Mac. "Your momma git some real affliction for you."

Carlos massaged his forehead with his free hand. "That's one way of putting it," he said, sighing. "My family does care, but you could also say that my affliction has arrived early."

It was a cloudless afternoon, and although it wasn't especially hot, the sun was uncompromising, bleaching the billboards, the outfield grass and Sonny DeMarco's face. Carlos had seen this pallid countenance in pitchers before, and it didn't inspire confidence.

The issue was Sonny's pitch count. He kept getting behind hitters and had to battle back to get hitters out, causing his pitch count to rise. He was also beginning to throw with his arm instead of properly leveraging his legs and hips. It was only the bottom of the fourth inning, and he had already given up three runs and had runners on first and second, with one out. The Knights had yet to score.

Carlos flashed two fingers, showing a curveball. *Sonny's got to mix this up, or we'll never get out of this inning*, thought Carlos.

Carlos glanced at the hitter, Toby Hall. He was a little taller than Carlos, but easily outweighed him by fifty pounds. *All right, big fella. Just swing and miss. That's all I'm asking.*

Sonny nodded. He wound up and delivered the pitch, lengthening his stride slightly. *It doesn't look right*, thought Carlos. *It seems….*

"Oh, crap!" he exclaimed.

The ball came in at the wrong speed with little spin, causing it to hang over the plate. Toby had his body weight back, and a slight hesitation allowed him to make direct contact with the ball. Carlos watched the ball sail over Sonny's head, rising into the desert sky until it crossed the outfield and landed in the center field stands.

A buzz went through the crowd. The umpire on the field pointed his index finger in the air, twirling it to indicate a home run.

"That'll do it for you, Sonny," said Carlos under his breath.

He stood up to take the pressure off his knees and watched the base runners make their way around the infield. Coach Capra stepped out of the dugout and slowly made his way to the mound with Big Mac not far behind.

You were nibbling, said Carlos to himself, following in the coach's footsteps. *Poor bastard, his mustache is twitching. Not a great way to start Spring training.*

"You're getting too cute," said Coach Capra, taking the ball from Sonny's hand. He glanced at Big Mac and Carlos, who were assembled at the mound. "I want to be clear to all of you. No more nibbling. The umpire's calling for a tight strike zone. Go directly after the hitter with your best stuff."

He handed the ball to Big Mac and stared at the stands in the outfield. "Man, Toby crushed that ball," said Coach Capra, more to himself than to the others.

Sonny stared at his feet dejectedly.

"Anyway, chin up, fellas. Let's return the favor after we get the hell out of this inning. All right?" Coach Capra patted Sonny on the shoulder and nodded at Carlos. "You got this," he said, walking away from the mound and toward the dugout.

"Don't worry," Big Mac said, "I'll git us out of this pickle. Don't worry."

About twenty minutes had passed since Coach Capra made the substitution for Big Mac, and the inning was no closer to ending. Carlos could tell that Big Mac was getting increasingly frustrated, his confidence cratering. The Bulls had added another four runs to their lead, keaving the Knights trailing ten to nothing.

To make matters worse, Carlos could hear Javier and Chucho in the stands, running a nonstop color commentary. "Just throw a strike, man!" shouted Javier, for the fourth or fifth time.

"Yeah, throw a strike, man," added Chucho while chewing a soft pretzel. "We're gonna be late for dinner!"

Wonderful, thought Carlos. *We're down in the count again, with a man on first and third, and I get to listen to this all afternoon.*

Carlos glanced at Jedediah Evans. He was a lanky contact hitter with excellent bat control. Just the type of hitter you wanted to avoid when your pitcher was cracking under pressure. Carlos sighed and made a signal for a fastball down the middle. *You must overpower him. He's not going to chase it out of the zone.*

Big Mac nodded, his face bright red from exertion, and began his wind up.

Easy does it. Doesn't have to be piping hot.

Big Mac strode forward and released the ball.

It's got good speed. It's moving a lot—

"What the hell!" shouted Jedediah, flinging the bat toward the first base line as he lurched backwards.

"You suck!" shouted someone from the stands.

"Can we get our money back?"

Carlos stood up and jogged toward the pitching mound. Big Mac was staring at the ground, kicking the mound with his cleats. "Big Mac, look," said Carlos. "This team is loaded, and it's just not our day. Just focus, and we can get out of this jam, all right?"

"I'm plumb flustrated, Carlos."

"Yeah, I can see that."

"Coach should just pull me."

Carlos stepped closer to Big Mac and glanced over toward the dugout. "You just need one or two more pitches to end this. Your fastball is working better for you today. That was just a frustration pitch."

Big Mac grunted and kicked the dirt on the mound in Carlos' direction. Carlos glanced at his clay-coated shin guards.

"I didn't mean to kick dirt at youse," said Big Mac, apologetically. "I aim to finish this up. I just needed a breather."

"Okay, good," said Carlos. "Fastball. Again, but down the middle."

Big Mac nodded, and Carlos jogged back to home plate. *Okay, Big Mac. Just focus,* thought Carlos as he got back into his crouch. Carlos looked up at Jedediah, who had a scowl on his face. Carlos inhaled deeply and made the sign for a fastball. *Come on now. Focus!* pleaded Carlos silently.

There was a thud of ball against jersey and flesh. The fastball hit Jedediah on the left shoulder. Carlos placed his mitt over his mask.

"Ye-ouch!" Jedediah shouted. "You stupid idiot! That was on purpose!"

Someone threw a hotdog from the stands toward home plate.

"I should beat your sorry ass!" shouted Jedediah, taking a step menacingly toward the pitching mound.

"No need to argy!" replied Big Mac angrily. "Bring it on, then!"

"Hey!" shouted the umpire. "Hey! None of that!"

Jedediah stared at the umpire and seemed to contemplate his options.

"Fight! Fight! Fight!" chanted a scattered assortment of spectators from the stands, which may have included Javier and Chucho.

Jedediah composed himself and smiled sinisterly, flipping his bat on the ground as he made his way to first base.

About five minutes later, Boo was standing on the mound, tossing a few warm-up pitches to Carlos before facing the next batter, Frankie "Tiny" Longo. Any player in baseball with the name of "Tiny" is not what you would describe as a bunting specialist. This was a matchup of power against power.

Carlos watched Tiny step up to the plate, holding the bat like a toothpick.

With the bases loaded, this is not the time for your eephus pitch, Boo, thought Carlos. *Fastball inside is what I want.*

A blaring, cacophony of trumpet sounds rang out. Carlos glanced at the stands near the first base line and saw ushers passing out plastic vuvuzelas. He could make out his mother and father, cheeks puffed out, as they blew the horns along with others in the crowd.

Carlos made the signal for the fastball. Boo spat in acknowledgement and began his complicated wind-up motion.

The horns blared louder, and Carlos thought he could see Boo's eyes dart toward the stands momentarily.

If you've ever cut down a large tree, you might know certain safety protocols around the fall path. There are critical signs to be aware of, such as listening for the cracking sound when the chainsaw has cut through most of the wood. At this point, it's advisable to stand on the opposite side of the falling tree, unless you don't have any plans for the rest of your life.

Boo's fastball produced a similar felling scenario. It was both fast and inside as Carlos had instructed. However, it was a bit *too* inside and much lower than expected, likely due to the distracting vuvuzelas. The ball rocketed straight into Tiny's protective manhood cup, causing the fans to gasp and quickly go silent. As far as Carlos could tell, Tiny didn't seem to react much at all, at first. He looked at the ball on the ground beside his feet, then looked at Boo, then down at his feet again, before slowly leaning forward and planting his face on the ground.

What happened next is best described as an eruption. Jedediah sprinted from first base toward the pitcher's mound, full of fury and lack of forethought. Boo dropped his glove, and Jedidiah launched into some sort of Taekwondo jump kick. Boo grabbed his legs in midair, spun him around and tossed him back toward first base. Jedediah landed awkwardly on his bruised shoulder, several feet from the pitcher's mound, causing him to cry out in pain and writhe on the ground. This caused the benches to clear, and soon there was a general melee on the field.

Big Mac was one of the first in on the action, riding piggyback on Toby Hall while slapping him on the head. Coach Kirk was arguing with the opposing pitching coach but was soon knocked over by a stampede of his own players. Jecito was engaged in an elaborate boxing match with a Bulls player, which involved plenty of defensive side-to-side steps and jabs in the air, but no actual punches.

The stadium roared with vuvuzelas and shouting. Carlos tried to break up a wrestling match between several players near home plate, but soon found himself sitting on top of a Bulls player doing a camel clutch move to pin his opponent down. To his horror, he saw his mother rushing through the field, swinging her purse at Bulls players like a battle ax. Unable to relinquish his current position lest his opponent gain the upper hand, he watched his mother swing her satchel at the Bulls general manager, causing him to lose his hat and stare dumbfoundedly at the female aggressor.

When stadium security finally entered the scene, most of the players were contorted in some sort of unnatural position on the ground, gasping for breath or groaning. The umpires were in a huddle near Boo, who was sitting on the pitching mound serenely chewing dip next to Carlos' mother, who was now filing her nails. Beside them were four Bulls players who were lying on their sides, holding one or more limbs in pain.

Later that afternoon, the Knights were gathered in the locker room around Coach Capra after losing to the Bulls fifteen to one. Most of the players had yet to change out of their jerseys because Coach Capra had called for an immediate after-action conference. Carlos was sitting on a bench next to Sonny, who was holding an ice pack against his right cheekbone.

"I'll just say this once," started Coach Capra. "That was a truly embarrassing performance. Really, a disgrace to the jerseys on your backs."

Carlos stared at Coach Kirk, lying in a supine position on a medical cot a couple of feet away, being attended to by the team's physician. He had bandages on his legs and back from cleat injuries and a cold cranial cap on his head to prevent swelling.

The room was silent, players dejectedly staring at their feet. There was a slightly audible "Mhmhfff" sound every so often from the direction of Coach Kirk.

"But I will say this…" Coach Capra rubbed his chin, pausing to find the right words. "Who the heck was that woman swinging the purse?"

Carlos felt eyes on him. He scanned the room to find Jecito, Big Mac, Sonny, Sean and Boo all staring at him. "Um… well…" began Carlos, his chest constricting with tension.

"Yes?" encouraged Coach Capra.

"Well, you see…"

"Spit it out, son."

"That was my mother."

"*Your mother?*"

"Yes, I'm afraid so."

"Mhmhfff."

"There, there," said Coach Capra, patting Coach Kirk roughly on the bandaged thigh.

Carlos noticed Boo was grinning, his eyes gleaming with an energy that he had never seen before.

"I don't suppose she's single?" asked Coach Capra.

"No, not single," said Carlos. "And fiercely loyal, if you didn't happen to notice."

"Right, right," said Coach Capra. "Well, you're lucky to have her on your side. Anyway, you're all dismissed. We gotta put this in the rearview mirror."

The players scattered, grabbing their street clothes from the lockers.

"Oh, Carlos," said Coach Capra, "come to my office, will you?"

Carlos met Coach Capra in the small office suite used by the coaching staff, which consisted of two rectangular faux-leather sofas, a coffee table, a large flat-screen TV affixed to the wall and an L-shaped, mahogany computer desk tucked away in the corner. Coach Capra was leaning against the wall and motioned for Carlos to sit on the sofa across from him.

"If this is about my mother, I apologize. It won't happen again," said Carlos, plopping into the sofa's squishy cushions.

"What's that?" said Coach Capra distractedly. "Never mind that. I wanted to discuss another matter."

Carlos twiddled his thumbs nervously. *I was assured a roster spot*, Carlos told himself unconvincingly.

"Carlos, do you know why we brought you here?"

"We discussed getting through to Boo."

"Yes, that's right," Coach Capra confirmed.

"It's still a work in progress. I haven't had much time to work with him."

"Yes, that's true."

Carlos continued, "I mean, today was a disaster. I don't think Boo was the main issue. I need to work with him on his control. I have some ideas–"

"Look, son," interrupted Coach Capra. "You're, first of all, a good player."

Carlos exhaled and leaned back into the sofa.

"You're a veteran. You've been around the league for a while. We brought you in to be a leader."

Coach Capra placed his hands on his hips and stared at Carlos. Carlos said nothing.

"What transpired today on the field, however, was a failure of leadership."

"But coach, the Bulls started it!"

"Nonsense. This has nothing to do with the Bulls," said Coach Capra sternly. "As I was saying, today was a setback. I take full responsibility for it. What I'm asking of you is to partner with me on this leadership journey."

Carlos nodded. No coach had ever phrased leadership in this way to him. *Partner with the coaching staff?*

"What you did today was disappointing. You were either too passive, allowing the Bulls hitters to get into the heads of our pitchers, or you were too aggressive, joining in on the brawl. That's not how leaders lead. I want you to be *assertive*. That means proactively working with the pitchers, like I've seen you do in practice, to encourage them to be the best versions of themselves. To calm them down. To guide them through the storms. That means speaking up in the locker room and on the field. That means calling the right pitches at the right time. That means working the umpires. That means controlling the game, because, unlike the coaching staff, you're the one in the game. And that means being above the fray, even when your emotions are trying to get the better of you."

Coach Capra pushed up the glasses on his nose, walked over to Carlos and placed his hand on his shoulder. "I know I can count on you, son. Get some rest, and let's come back tomorrow ready to play ball."

The following week, Carlos was sitting at the bar with Big Mac, Jecito and Sean at the Coyote Saloon and Lounge on the south end of Oracle Road in Tucson. It was happy hour, but no one was in a festive mood.

"And just like that, I'm demoted to High-A. One bad outing and I'm done for," said Sean, who was at this point on his third beer.

"It was my nerves," added Jecito, who was also on his third beer. "They never got a chance to see my best stuff."

Big Mac was quiet and staring blankly at the TV screen, which was showing the White Sox playing the Padres. Paul Konerko had just stepped up to the plate.

"It's been a tough week," said Carlos.

"At least you're still on the roster," said Jecito. "But I'm happy for you, don't get me wrong."

"You can never feel secure in this game," said Carlos, taking another swig of beer.

"I feel like singing..." said Jecito, staring at the empty karaoke stage beside the bar.

"Singing is rooted in suffering," added Sean.

Carlos looked at Big Mac, who had five empty IPA bottles in front of him. His eyes were bloodshot.

"Come on, Big Mac, why don't you try karaoke?" said Carlos. "Screw the coaches. You'll land somewhere else, I'm sure."

Big Mac shook his head.

"Aspite all I'd done, I'm cut," moaned Big Mac. "What about loyalty? What about all the help I've given? It's all backards."

"That'll be Jäger bombs to go around," said a shadowy figure walking up to the bar.

Carlos turned around and saw Boo standing behind him, empty thirty-five-ounce beer mug in hand. "And give me an extra two shots for good measure," he added.

"Boo?" said Big Mac through bleary eyes. "From Oklihomi? Pirate of the Plains?"

"That's me," said Boo. "I'm sorry about the cuts, guys."

They all stared at Boo, with beer bottles halfway to their mouths. This was the most extensive conversation they'd had with him in all of Spring training.

"Good to see you, Boo," said Carlos at last. "Looks like you're all that's left of the Mad Dawgz."

Boo grabbed a barstool and squeezed in between Carlos and Big Mac and placed the empty mug on the countertop. He was wearing a red linen bandana over his head, tied back in a knot so the two ends of the cloth fell down his neck. His long, tangled black hair spilled out from under the bandana over his bushy beard and shoulders.

He does look like a pirate, thought Carlos.

The bartender took away the empty mug, then passed out Jäger bombs.

"Cheers," said Boo, raising a shot glass, before downing all three of his in rapid succession.

Carlos stared at the Jäger bomb, hesitating for a moment. *I'm not sure this is going to end well*, he thought, but drank it anyway.

A few minutes later, they were gathered on the karaoke stage, singing "Last Resort" by Papa Roach. Carlos and Sean were bouncing up and down to the lyrics. Boo had unfurled his headband and was head-banging, while Jecito and Big Mac were shouting into the microphone the chorus line:

"Wish somebody would tell me I'm fine!
Nothing's all right, nothing is fine
I'm running and I'm crying
I'm crying, I'm crying..."

There was an awkward silence after the song ended, with most of the patrons heading for the exit. "That was awful," said one patron.

"Seriously, that was a horrible performance," said another.

"My hearing is permanently damaged," said someone else.

"I love you guys!" said Jecito, ignoring the audience feedback.

"Mad Dawgz forever!" cried Big Mac. "I lerve you too!"

"Should we play it again?" asked Boo.

A few days later, the Knights were holding bullpen pitching drills during an off day, and Carlos was standing near third base with his glove extended in the air in front of Boo. The purpose of the exercise was for the pitchers to simulate their pitching motions, striking the dangling gloves at the proper release point with a towel. Coach Kirk and other members of the staff were making the rounds among the players, inspecting the pitching mechanics, and providing feedback.

They were about fifteen minutes into the drill when Carlos noticed something unusual in Boo's delivery... something even more unusual than normal about his delivery. After about the first dozen repetitions of the drill, the whip of the towel and Boo's release point diverged. It was a subtle change that became more pronounced the longer the drill went on.

He's not tired, thought Carlos. *He's built like a tractor.*

Carlos studied Boo as he progressed from his wind up, pivoting into his stride, with a towel in hand. Carlos stepped back and crossed his arms.

"What's going on?" asked Boo gruffly, whipping the towel into thin air.

"Your arm isn't aligned with your back," said Carlos. "Try it again now."

Boo glared at Carlos. He took a step back, exhaled and began his pitching motion again.

The towel hit Carlos's extended glove at his exact release point.

"Good!" said Coach Kirk, nodding at the two of them before hopping over to another group of players on his crutches.

"Not good," replied Carlos, after the coach was out of earshot.

"What do you mean?" asked Boo hotly, crossing his arms.

"When I was growing up, I always had trouble reading," said Carlos. "The letters and numbers looked backwards to me. I couldn't spell. Still can't spell, to be honest. I always thought I was dumb, and it didn't help having an older sister who was top of her class. A few years back I got tested and learned that I had dyslexia and ADHD. It was the best test I ever took. I started developing better habits. I learned new coping techniques. My batting average went up. My defense improved. My confidence as a player, as a person, grew. Tell me, Boo, has anyone ever said you have trouble staying focused?"

Boo narrowed his eyes and stared at Carlos.

"Listen, Boo, I don't mean to offend you–"

"Yeah," interrupted Boo, sighing. "Yeah, I've heard that refrain my entire life, now that you mention it."

"You get easily distracted?"

"That's right."

"You lose things?"

"Yeah."

"You're disorganized?"

"Yeah."

"Disheveled?"

"Come on, man that's part of my look!"

"You can't sustain your attention? You lose steam as you pitch? Even during your windups?"

"Damn. Is it that bad?"

Carlos walked over to Boo and placed his hand on his shoulder.

"There's hope, my friend. The last drill you did was perfect. But it was perfect because I got you to focus again. I have an idea."

On Saturday, Art Sanders was scheduled to start against the Durham Bulls. It was a rematch, their first game since the brawl. The coaching staff had been preparing the team for the series, emphasizing execution and revisiting film.

Carlos had fully bought into the game plan. He also had a migraine from a night out with Boo. These were complimentary issues. He wanted to execute better, and he also needed to foster a closer relationship with the erratic pitcher. When the telephone blared in his room, he fell to the floor in a fetal position but managed to compose himself and reach for it.

"Uh-huh," muttered Carlos into the receiver.

"Carlos. It's Coach," said Coach Capra. "I need you at the field in thirty minutes. We have a situation."

"Say what?" asked Carlos, glancing at the clock. It was ten o'clock in the morning.

"That's right. We have a situation. Easier to explain in person," said Coach Capra curtly before hanging up the phone.

About thirty minutes later, Carlos found Coach Capra in his office at the stadium. He was sitting on one of the two leather sofas in the room, across from Coach Kirk and Coach Bowers.

"He's had his chances. Let's get some new arms in there," said Coach Kirk.

"I think I've seen enough as well. I agree with Kirk," said Coach Bowers.

"Ah, good, you're here," said Coach Capra, looking up at the doorway and waving Carlos in. "Come in, son."

Carlos stepped into the office and stood beside Coach Kirk. His crutches were leaning against the armrest of the sofa.

"Sit down," said Coach Capra, motioning to his sofa. "Look, we have a situation and I want to talk it through as a leadership team."

Coach Kirk frowned. Carlos wasn't sure if he shared Coach Capra's view about his leadership credentials or if the past several weeks had just resulted in a general malaise for the pitching coach. Carlos thought he was looking better, with his head bandages being removed, but he still was wearing a walking boot for his ankle injured during the melee.

"Art's not going to pitch today," said Coach Capra. "He's got the flu."

"I see," said Carlos. "He's had a good Spring training,"

"I would agree," replied Coach Capra. "I'd like to have Boo start. But it's a matter of some debate here. My thought is that we should see what he's got left in the tank."

"Like I said, Nick," said Coach Bowers, "we've seen enough. Boo's been around the league and isn't showing signs of improvement. I suggest we bring in some of our other prospects."

"That's the thing, Rob," countered Coach Capra. "I think we *have* seen signs of improvement. You're looking at a *sign* right now!"

Coach Kirk and Coach Bowers glanced at Carlos. Carlos swallowed and shifted uneasily in his seat.

"The White Sox desperately need pitching. Boo's played in the big leagues and could still provide value if called up," said Coach Capra, turning to Carlos. "I've seen you working with him. You're communicating better. What do you think, son?"

Carlos thought about the bullpen pitching drills. "Boo can pitch just fine," said Carlos. "He should start."

"And what makes you so confident, given recent evidence to the contrary?" asked Coach Bowers.

"From personal experience, I can attest to the fact that he doesn't recognize boundaries with the strike zone," added Coach Kirk, mournfully.

"Coach is right. I've been communicating a lot better with Boo lately. His issue isn't control. I mean, not in the traditional sense," Carlos added quickly, glancing at Coach Kirk. "His issue is focus."

"Go on," said Coach Capra.

"Well, I noticed during practice that Boo's accuracy suffers the longer he's going through drills. It's not fatigue. His eyes start to wander, and his entire pitching motion gets out of sync. It's subtle, but I could tell because I have the same challenges myself. I don't think he's ever been tested, but I swear he's got ADHD. There are some tricks we can try during the game to keep his head in it. I have confidence in him. He should start."

Coach Capra stood up and placed his arms behind his back. He stared into the distance for a moment, lost in thought.

"I'm making an executive decision," Coach Capra announced at last. "Boo's going to start. If he runs into trouble, we pull him."

Álvaro García-Gómez was a nineteen-year-old player from Santo Domingo who had been terrorizing minor league hitters for the past year. At five-foot-eleven and one-hundred-and-seventy pounds, he wasn't an imposing figure, but his lightning-fast arm more than made up for brute force. He was a sharp contrast to Boo. He was a cerebral pitcher who seemed able to assess a batter's swing speed in the moment and adjust accordingly. His attention to detail, feel for the game and his ability to maintain his composure, even in the middle of a jam, was unusual for a player his age.

Carlos had faced him last year and wanted nothing to do with him. This game was Boo's last chance to prove himself, and going up against Alvaro wasn't encouraging. If Boo was cut, Carlos wasn't sure where he would stand with the club. He suspected Double-A.

Carlos and Boo had just completed their pre-game routine and were huddled in the bullpen with Big Mac, who was holding a bugle. The game was about to start.

"Big Mac, I owe you," said Carlos.

"I'm mighty fond of you'ns," he said. "Boo's the last Mad Dawgz standing."

"You really think this will work?" asked Boo.

"I sure hope so," said Carlos. "When you hear the cue, you know what to do, right?"

"Yeah, I got it," said Boo.

"Good. Well, let's show this kid what veteran *hombres* are really like," said Carlos, swatting him on the chest with his glove. "You got this, Boo. I believe in you."

What makes the eephus pitch one of the most confounding pitches for hitters is that everyone knows it's coming. You can disguise the pitch, but once it pops seven feet in the air and wobbles down toward home plate, most hitters can't seem to adjust. The angles and movement seem all wrong, and aggressive hitters rarely have the patience to wait for the ball to come into striking range.

The Durham Bulls, through the first three innings, were eager to punish Boo after the last brawl, but kept getting baited by the high-arching ball that seemed to glide on the wind like a kite. When sprinkled with his fastball, which was all but a blur to the Bulls, Boo struck out the hapless hitters so quickly during the first three innings that Carlos hardly had to employ his "special" tactics. There was one instance when Boo was distracted by a heckler in the stands, and Carlos flapped his arms to get his attention. Boo subsequently threw a 103-mph fastball down the middle of the plate, which was just the response Carlos wanted.

Unfortunately, Álvaro similarly befuddled the Knights, striking out the hitters through the first three innings as well. His repertoire was more sophisticated and included a four-seam fastball, a two-seam fastball, a power curveball, a knuckleball and a circle changeup. With both clubs agreeing to shorten the game to seven innings prior to the match, Carlos thought he might be heading home before rush hour.

In the fourth inning, Boo faced the top of the order again. Carlos watched Jedediah Evans step up to the plate and thought he looked tentative. The last outing had not gone well for him at the plate.

Carlos smiled and inched closer to Jedediah. "You're gonna get a fastball," said Carlos.

"What's that?" replied Jedidiah, glancing at Carlos nervously while wagging his bat in the air.

"Just wanted to let you know that you're gonna see a fastball, inside."

Jedidiah glanced again at Carlos, while attempting to keep his eye on the ball.

"You trying to be smart?" retorted Jedidiah.

"STRIKE!" shouted the umpire.

"Sheeeee…" groaned Jedidiah, looking at the umpire, then at Carlos.

"Just wanted to let you know what's coming."

"Now, you just shut it," cried Jedidiah. "You just tell your pitcher to keep the ball over the plate. I want no more of those wild pitches hitting my shoulder."

"Yeah, understood," said Carlos. "Anything else? I can have him throw a fastball, just outside if you like."

"Listen, now. You're being a smartass."

Carlos looked at Boo. *No need to take any chances with the pitches veering in the wrong direction*, he thought. *Let's make sure he knows exactly what to do.*

"Hey, Boo!" shouted Carlos. "Fastball, outside corner of the plate!"

Carlos didn't bother making the sign for the pitch. Boo nodded and went through his delivery motion.

Jedidiah swatted at the air.

"STRIKE!" shouted the umpire.

Jedidiah's knees were twitching now. The sound of the ball hitting Carlos' glove seemed to affect him.

"That must have been his fastest pitch of the day," said Carlos to Jedidiah. "He's been clocked at 105, you know?"

Jedidiah said nothing. Carlos noticed he had moved to the far edge of the batter's box as he got back into his batting stance.

"Boo, go easy on him, will you?!" shouted Carlos, not bothering to make the sign for the pitch.

Boo nodded and began his wind up. He launched a high, looping ball that moved a foot in each direction before landing on home plate and bouncing into the crumpled Jedidiah, who had fallen after wildly swinging at the pitch before it was within reach.

"OUT!" shouted the umpire.

Trev Nicholson was up next. He was the Bulls' backup shortstop and utility man and had been around the league for years. Carlos had played against him in High-A, but their paths hadn't crossed for many years. He was one of those crafty journeymen who had survived in the minors, occasionally making cameos in the big league when teams were in a bind.

Carlos made the signal for a fastball, inside. Boo wiped the sweat from his forehead with the back of his sleeve and nodded. He began his delivery motion and launched a ball, right on the edge of the plate. Trev held his ground, making no attempt to hit it.

"BALL!" shouted the umpire.

"Hey, now," said Carlos, turning to the umpire behind him. "That was definitely a strike."

"I called ball," said the umpire. "It was low and outside. Ball it is."

"Okey-dokey, sir," said Carlos, swallowing his pride. "We'll be mindful of that next time."

Trev smirked and tapped the barrel of his bat on the plate.

"I see what y'all are doing," said Trev under his breath to Carlos. "Not going to work on me. Boo never makes it beyond four innings."

Carlos ignored his feedback and raised his glove momentarily over his head to get Boo's attention, before bringing it down and making the signal for a fastball, outside. In the stands near the dugout, there was a slight commotion after someone spilled their beer. Boo's eyes darted momentarily to the crowd as he went through his windup. His release and momentum were off, and he missed right and low. Trev showed a bunt, but quickly pulled back.

"BALL!"

Come on, Boo, you got this, said Carlos to himself.

"Try hitting this," said Carlos to Trev, signaling for the eephus pitch.

Boo went through his delivery and threw the high-looping pitch. Trev stood still as the ball landed in Carlos' glove outside the strike zone.

"BALL!"

Oh boy, thought Carlos. *You're pitching great. Don't lose focus now!*

Carlos stood up as he tossed the ball back to Boo. Then, glancing in the stands near first base, he pointed his glove toward Big Mac. Big Mac waved and raised his bugle.

Carlos got back into his stance and made the sign for a fastball, down the middle. At this point, a high-pitched song of reveille blared from the stands, reminiscent of a call for Union cavalry, ending with a small crowd clapping and shouting "Charge!"

Boo smiled and threw a fastball down the middle, slightly low, causing Trev to swing and clip the top of the ball. The ball bounced in front of home plate, rolling toward the third base line.

Carlos leapt to his feet, snatched the ball and tossed it to first base for an easy out.

"That's how we do it!" shouted Carlos to Boo.

Chase Cunningham was up next, and Carlos motioned to Bic Mac in the stands again. The call of the cavalry rang out, with the crowd getting more enthusiastic about the battle cry. The bugle energized Boo as well, and he tossed the same pitch three times in a row, causing Chase to promptly strike out and end the inning.

"I tell you what," said Carlos to Boo as they walked to the dugout, "I think you just threw a splitter."

"You think so?"

"The bottom fell off the ball, so I'd called it one."

Coach Capra walked over to Boo and patted him on the back. "Nice work, you two," he said, as they took their seats on the benches. "I would agree with Carlos. Looks like you've got more pitches up your sleeve than you realize."

"That bugle call really gets me going," said Boo.

"Yeah, energizes me, too," Carlos agreed.

"I don't know what the heck you guys are talking about," said Coach Capra, "but just keep doing what you're doing. We need the very best of you to survive Álvaro."

Surviving Álvaro was much easier said than done. His fastball and his changeup were unhittable and seemed to make hitters spin like a dreidel. The top of the Knights' order was soon spiraling their way back to the dugout, dispirited, and before Carlos and Boo could get much of a breather, they were back on the field.

"Good grief," cried Coach Kirk, putting his head in his hands, "that Álvaro makes it look so easy!"

Holden Powell was first up at bat. He was a line-drive hitter and rarely struck out, with the exception being his earlier outing. He stepped into the batter's box, taking a couple of practice swings before settling into his batter's stance.

Carlos got down behind him, twirling his hand in the air to signal the reveille call. There was no response. He twirled his hand in the air again, but there was still no response.

"Okay, cut this nonsense out," said the umpire.

Carlos glanced over his shoulder and noticed a minor fracas in the stands. Big Mac was trying to grab his bugle from a much larger man, who was holding it up in the air. Carlos thought the man looked like Tiny Longo, but he wasn't sure.

Carlos signaled for a fastball, outside. A moment later there was a cracking sound as Holden's bat split in two, sending the barrel of the bat toward first base while the ball sailed over second base for a single. Out of the corner of his eye, Carlos noticed a glittering metal object fly over the stadium railing and land near the first base coach's box.

"Dang it. The bugle was really working," muttered Carlos.

The next batter, Alfonso Correa, stepped into the batter's box. He had been involved in the brawl at their last match and had made the mistake of trying to wrestle Boo.

Back to basics, thought Carlos. *He's losing steam.*

"Boo, fastball, down the middle!" he shouted.

That should get Boo's mind back into the game.

A few seconds later, Carlos watched the ball soar into deep left center field for a double. Holden made it to third and was a quarter of the way home, before turning back for safety.

Carlos walked over to the mound to have a conversation with Boo.

"How are you feeling, Boo?" asked Carlos.

"Fine."

"Kind of surprised Alfonso got a hit off you after what happened at our last game."

"You mean him trying to body slam me?"

"Yeah, that."

"Amateur move."

"That's what I think."

"You know, I just had him in a headlock. It was your mother who finished him off."

"I see. I wasn't aware of that."

"That's right. I had his head in my arm and was still deciding what to do with him, when *whack!* your mom hit him over the head with her purse. He was out cold."

"Yikes. I should really apologize to him."

"Never saw it coming. Still has no idea what hit him."

"Amazing, really."

"It was. I love your mother. We bonded on the mound that day," Boo looked toward the box seats behind home plate. "By the way, is the next signal a drum? These musical instruments are very inspiring. They help me focus, like I'm a member of the cavalry."

Carlos turned and saw Big Mac in one of the box seats carrying a marching bass drum. Big Mac waved his mallet, smiling.

"That should work," said Carlos, patting Boo on the butt with his glove. "You're playing great. Don't worry about the base runners, just focus on hitting your spots."

Timothy Rhodes stepped into the batter's box to the sonorous thumping of the bass drum. His subsequent line drive to first base and Rick Anderson's quick pivot and throw from first base to Carlos at home plate, resulted in a near collision with Holden, who was tagged out.

Double plays are a pitcher's best friend and have a demoralizing effect on the opposition. The next Bulls' hitter, Mark Jackson, lasted only a single at bat, popping the ball up in the air toward Boo and quickly ending the inning.

At the bottom of the seventh inning, Guillermo Sandoval was up for the Knights in the middle of the order. There were two outs and no runners on base. Neither team had scored a run yet.

Carlos was sitting next to Sonny and Boo in the dugout, chewing sunflower seeds. He spat his shells on the ground in the time-honored tradition of making every attempt to clog the drains. "They should let you guys finish duking it out," said Sonny to Boo.

"Coach said the game's over after this inning, no matter the score," said Boo.

"It's a shame, really," said Carlos. "Best game of your career, and you don't get a win. Not that it would have been recorded in the official stat sheets."

They turned their attention to the field as Guillermo fouled his first pitch.

"Come on, G, you can do it," encouraged Sonny.

"Statement game, though," said Carlos to Boo. "What more could they ask of you?"

Boo spat a sunflower shell on the ground.

"You always got a chance with a jersey on your back," said Boo. "I pitched for the White Sox a few times before I blew out my elbow."

"Never knew that," said Carlos.

"Tommy John surgery set me back. Had trouble with my control afterwards."

"STRIKE!" shouted the umpire.

There was a crashing sound nearby, and turning their heads toward the dugout steps, they saw Big Mac unload his bass drum on the ground while gingerly trying to prevent his beer from spilling outside his plastic cup.

"Apparently the Mad Dawgz are still in the house!" shouted Big Mac, as he high-fived his way through the dugout to Carlos.

"They didn't give you any trouble coming down here, did they?" asked Carlos, giving Big Mac the secret Mad Dawgz dap, which included a chest bump and spilt beer.

"No trouble at all. They hired me, as a matter of fact. Coach offered me a job, just a few minutes ago."

"Are you serious?" asked Carlos.

"Well, I may not be book read or all biggety like some of them coaches, but I know a thing or two about working hard. And yessiree, I have myself a job as assistant strength and conditioning coach."

Sonny dropped his bag of sunflower seeds on the ground.

"BALL!" shouted the umpire.

"Strength and conditioning, you said? You?" cried Sonny, staring at the Big Mac's sleeveless West Virginia Mountaineers basketball jersey, which was noticeably protruding from his midsection.

"I was a little surprised, but Coach said something about needing a more relatable member of his staff."

"Yeah, I can see that," said Carlos.

"I guess our conditioning doesn't usually work up a sweat," said Sonny.

"That's right," said Boo. "You'll fit right back in. You'll be a player coach."

"I'll tell you'ns something," said Big Mac, taking a sip of his beer. "Dat was a heck of a game."

"BALL!" shouted the umpire.

"Never seen you work the umpire so much, Carlos. I could hear you messin' with the Bulls' hitters. It was a masterpiece, the way you managed the game."

Big Mac scratched his armpit thoughtfully.

"BALL!" shouted the umpire.

"Boo, I'm a-fixin' to make sure they don't think a cutting you. I mean, you were dominant. The entire Bulls lineup, the whole kit an' kaboodle, couldn't do nothing but spin on 'er heels tryin' to hit you."

"I appreciate it, Big Mac."

"I had anudder job offer," added Big Mac. "The Cleveland Symphony offered me ta play second violinist."

"The what?!" cried Carlos, Sonny and Boo at the same time.

"I dabbled with various instruments in my day," said Big Mac.

"I can see that!" said Carlos.

"It's just different, playing ball. For all the crap, and there is *a lot* of crap we deal with ina minors, there's somepin' to be said about the thrill of the chase. You may not think you're gonna make it. You may wanna quit. You may even git cut. But if you keep your eye ona ball and give it all you got, you can 'complish great things, even if that foul ball you just hit takes your life in a different die-rection than ya thought."

"STRIKE!" shouted the umpire. "GAME OVER!"

"Couldn't have said it better, Big Mac," replied Carlos. "Or should we say, Coach Mac?"

"Coach Big Mac?" added Sonny.

"Look, fellas. As far as I'm concerned, it's alla same," said Big Mac. "Long as I'm nigh you, long as I'm nigh this game, long as I kin smell the pine tar, feel the seams on the ball, taste the sunflower seeds and even chew dat nasty dip, I'll be happy as a pig in muck. Life's too short to waste on things dat bring you no joy. It's a child's game, sure, but I think dat's why we love it so much. It takes us to a time when things was simpler, less stressful. And if we kin share dat youthful joy with our fans, if we kin help bring people to-gether, make 'em smile and laugh, take 'em away from com-puters and gadgets an' distractions, an' let 'em experience the simple satisfaction of being present with the people they love, what better gift is there? It's a public service ta play this game, and I'm honored ta serve ya and the fans of this team, through the ups and downs and everythin' in between as we get ready to start the regular season."

THE VISITORS

Six-year-old Luna Burgos kneeled in the hallway of her grandparents' house next to a towering, ticking grandfather clock, wearing green pajamas with the hood pulled over her head so she looked like an oversized frog. Behind her were Benjamin, her older brother, and her two first cousins, Ricky and Zoe Burgos, similarly dressed in fleece pajamas of varying colors and sizes.

It was a quarter to midnight, on the eve of Three Kings Day, and they were up past their bedtime. Luna's father had told her that since her house was full of guests, it would be good for Luna and Benjamin to spend some time with Abuela and Abuelo, who lived only fifteen minutes away.

"You can also play with your cousins," he said. "You don't see them very often."

Luna could hardly contain her excitement at seeing them. She had waited all day for them to arrive. But her aunt, uncle and cousins hadn't landed at O'Hare until four o'clock in the afternoon, which seemed like an eternity for her. And Benjamin was no company, playing by himself on his stupid Game Boy. She knew she shouldn't swear, especially on the eve of such a holy day, but the games he played *were* stupid, especially since they never involved her, which was unfair.

And because of her age, Papi did not let her have a Game Boy either. That was just unfair, because she was in first grade and could do *both* addition and subtraction.

Luna would have brooded about her brother's behavior had it not been for an incident shortly before her cousins arrived. She was sitting by herself on her bed in one of the guest bedrooms, coloring Cinderella's dress pink in a coloring book, when the doorbell rang. It was cold outside, and she could hear the wind whistling through the narrow gangway separating her grandparents' aging three-flat from the one next door. Then she heard the front door slam shut and she leapt off the bed in fright.

"*Sí, está bien. No te preocupes,*" she heard Abuela say to someone not to worry.

"He'll be fine," said Abuelo. "Come in, please, don't cry."

Luna was standing near the edge of the bed, with several crayons scattered close to her feet. Curiosity getting the best of her, Luna tiptoed to the bedroom door, which was partially open, and peered into the hallway. Abuela was leading a woman and a young man into the master bedroom.

The young man was tall and slightly hunched, with wide-set eyes, a broad face and a flat nose. He had black hair cut in a bowl shape, like a mushroom, and he was wearing an unzipped, oversized gray winter parka, blue jeans and black sneakers. He was moaning, swaying his head and shoulders back and forth, and appeared inconsolable.

"He's having an episode," said the woman as she entered the bedroom.

A moment later, Luna saw Abuelo hurrying into the bedroom with a steaming mug of something in his hands.

The moaning continued, and Luna thought she could hear the woman crying. After a few minutes, she stepped into the hallway and walked toward the guest bedroom, in the opposite direction of the master bedroom, intent on asking Benjamin about those strange visitors.

"Benjamin!" she whispered, but he had his headphones on and was lost in his game. "Benjamin!" she said again in a hushed voice, sitting next to him on the edge of the bed. The acknowledgement never came.

"Ouch!" cried Benjamin, taking off his headphones and rubbing his arm. "You pinched me!"

"Shh!" Luna hissed, pressing her index finger to her lips. "Something's happening in the next room."

"You made me fall into a pit! Leave me alone!" he yelled, shoving her off the bed.

"Ah, forget it!" she huffed, pulling herself off the floor.

Luna turned around and went to the master bedroom, then crouched down beside the doorframe and craned her head so she could see her grandparents and the strangers inside.

"He has been like this since we came back from PR," said the woman, wringing her hands, tears rolling down her cheeks. "It's been two days. Sometimes he's fine, but then his episodes start again. Please..."

"Hush now." said Abuela, placing her hand on the man's chest, who was sitting on the edge of the bed with his jacket on the floor. He was twisting his head and neck, swinging it from side to side, while staring at the ceiling. Every so often, he made a clucking sound, like a chicken.

Luna felt her heart pounding in her chest. *What's happening?* she wondered. *What's wrong with him?*

Abuela walked over to a small wooden nightstand near her bed and pulled out a gold necklace with a cross pendant from a drawer. Holding the necklace in the air, she stood beside him and closed her eyes.

"Fly away!" she said in a soft but powerful voice. "Fly away now. I ask my *protecciones, Santa María, madre de*

Dios, to intercede on behalf of Álvaro López, son of Landrada López."

The clucking sound intensified, and in between gesticulations, the boy shouted profanities. Luna yelped in fright, and the visiting woman glanced at the door. Luna placed her hand in front of her mouth but was otherwise too terrified to move.

In a rising voice, Abuela exclaimed, "Shine a light on my spiritual *power. Ease the pain of this poor soul!*"

Abuela dropped the necklace onto the young man's lap. She then opened her eyes, grabbed his cheeks and forced him to stare into her eyes. The wind stopped howling outside, and Abuela's shadow seemed to spread along the floor in such a way that the silhouette of her arms resembled wings. The man looked at Abuela. His trance-like fever snapped, and he reached for her hands. A minute passed in silence, the man holding Abuela's hands, and Abuela holding the man by his cheeks. Somehow, the only word that popped into Luna's mind was *love*.

"She has magic powers!" whispered Luna to her brother and two cousins later that night.

"I bet she's a witch," Ricky said.

"There's no such thing!" Benjamin challenged him.

"I want to see her," Zoe added.

Luna then offered, "I bet her powers are strongest at midnight."

"That's nonsense!" said Benjamin in a superior tone; he was the oldest.

"We'll take a peek in her bedroom, see if she's changed," said Luna.

"Will it be dangerous?" asked Zoe.

"Abuela? Dangerous? No way," said Luna.

Giving Zoe's shoulder a slight push, Ricky said it was impossible.

"Ow! Stop that!" cried Zoe.

"Shh!" Luna and Benjamin said at the same time.

It was five minutes to midnight now, and the four children were on their hands and knees in the hallway, several feet away from their grandparents' door.

"So, where did the man and woman go?" Ricky asked.

"I don't know," Luna said. "After he got better, Abuelo gave him some tea, then they left."

"Do you think she'll ride a broomstick?" Zoe asked.

"I don't think she's like that," Luna said.

"What other types of witches are there?" asked Ricky.

"I don't know," Luna said. "She doesn't have a crooked nose or a big black hat."

Luna hopped toward her grandparents' door, peered in, and said, "All I know is that she's different."

The other children crawled over to the bedroom door and looked inside. Abuela was sleeping on her side at the edge of the bed, facing the door. Abuelo was on the other side of the bed, snoring. The lights from the streetlamps shone in through the windows and cast odd shadows.

"I don't think we should be here," Zoe whispered.

In a hushed voice, Ricky replied, "Don't be such a wuss."

The clock struck midnight, and a deep, resonant bell rang out across the hall, followed by another and another until the bell sounded twelve times. Luna gripped Benjamin's hand, staring into the room, her heart pounding again at being near Abuela.

And then Abuela opened one eye wide. Like chickens bursting from a coop at the sight of a fox, the children sprang up to their feet, knowing that they had no business being in Abuela's room. They ran back to their rooms and plunged under their covers, still shaking from seeing an eye that seemed to penetrate and scold their naughty souls. If they had listened carefully to something other than the chattering of their teeth and the rustling of their sheets, they might have heard a chuckle—or a cackling, who's to say for sure?—emanating from the master bedroom down the hall.

A WARNING

When César Aguilar was discharged from the army after having spent two tours in Iraq, he brought the war back with him to West Division Street. He was full of fury and paranoia, patrolling the neighborhood like he was still part of a mechanized infantry regiment.

You look suspicious. Bam! How do you like the taste of my baton?

Loitering on the street corner? Bam! Get your ass outta here!

Smoking dope? Bam! I just got the joint for you.

He was mad as hell, and anyone who had an ounce of sense steered clear of him. He was one of those cops who assumed that if you knew any gangbangers, then you had to be one yourself. Which meant that the entire neighborhood was a crime scene.

Now, don't get me wrong... Humboldt Park wasn't exactly Lake Forest, and there were reasons to want a little more law and order. I'll even go so far as to say that there were plenty of reasons to want to get crime under control, but César wasn't the answer.

What's ironic is that he was one of us. I knew him from elementary school. His mother was from Puerto Rico and had come to the States when he was two or three years old.

When César and I were in fifth grade, he became part of my inner circle. It was César, Andrés, Wilson and me. We called ourselves "CLAW," and we were like a gang, but in a nonviolent way. We looked out for each other and were teammates in sports and street games. César could run like a Ford Mustang, and no one could catch him in a race. We played on the same baseball team, and César stole so many bases, they called him "The Flash."

I'll never forget watching him sprint like a stallion, nostrils flared, eyes wide open, when the cops came by one night. We were in eighth grade, hanging out around the fire station on North Western Avenue. We had this game going where we'd accelerate on our skateboards from the fire station driveway until we reached the curb across the street. At that point, we'd try to leap from our boards, transition into a full sprint, then run up the brick wall of the nearby three-flat, trying to touch the highest point possible.

After about thirty minutes of this, a police cruiser came by, lights flashing, and screeched to a stop at the intersection near the fire station. We saw this fat, pasty police officer and his lanky sidekick get out of the cruiser, ready to lay down the law (whatever that was). So, doing what any sensible inner-city kid would under the circumstances, we scattered in every direction. César picked up his skateboard and ran up to the cops, gave them the finger, then sprinted down North Western Avenue and into the setting sun. It was pure poetry in motion.

That was about the last image I had of César as a kid. He ended up moving out of the neighborhood later that spring, and we didn't talk to each other again for years. Shortly before I started culinary school, I heard from Wilson that César had enlisted in the Army. It wasn't the first profession I had envisioned for César, but I thought that regardless, it would make good use of his athletic abilities.

César moved back to Chicago in 2007, retired from the Army as a master sergeant. My understanding was that besides being discharged, he had just gone through a nasty divorce, with his wife having contemplated filing a restraining order on him. By then, I was married for many years to Rebecca, with two teenagers, Benjamin and Luna, and had just moved the family from the city to the suburbs. Part of the motivation for the move was to get my children into a more academically rigorous school. My businesses had done well. I owned several small restaurants, and we could afford a new home in Morton Grove.

We had raised our kids in Wicker Park, a couple of miles east of my parents' home, and had enjoyed the trendy bars and cafés there. It wasn't an ideal place to start a family. It was overpriced but it was close to my parents. They were so entrenched in the community, for better or worse, that I suspected only a hearse would take them away from it.

Rebecca had wanted out of the city for some time. Her family lived in Skokie, and we felt cramped in our three-bedroom condominium. Most of all, she had this constant uneasiness about the crime that seemed to encroach from the west.

After we moved to Morton Grove, we would visit my parents on the weekends, usually on Sunday mornings, for brunch after Mass. My cousin Mercedes, her husband Javier, and their daughter Isabella lived close to our parents, and we would often see them as well. Occasionally, Mercedes, who owned a hair salon, would cut our family's hair.

One Sunday morning in February, on our way to Mass, my father brought up César. We were walking up the steps of Our Lady of Grace and St. Sylvester Parish when he placed his hand on my shoulder. "Luis, your friend César has moved back to the neighborhood."

"I'm sorry, who's that?" I asked, not having heard César's name in years. "César," he repeated. "Your friend who joined the Army."

"My friend who joined the Army?" I muttered to myself. "Yes, you used to play with César, Andrés and Wilson...."

"Oh, César Aguilar?" I asked, the memory of our boyhood crew, CLAW, coming back to me. "I haven't seen him in ages."

"Good," said my father. "Stay away from him."

A few months later, I was at Mercedes' salon on the corner of North Hamlin Avenue and West Thomas Street with Benjamin and his two friends, Tony and Noah. Benjamin was at that awkward teenage phase where grooming was still being figured out, and I wanted to get him a haircut. To motivate him to come with me to the salon, I suggested he bring Tony and Noah after their Monday afternoon basketball practice. It was Pulaski Day. Our community celebrated the Revolutionary War hero of Polish descent with a holiday and kids didn't have to go to school.

"We'll grab pizza and catch a movie," I said encouragingly.

The salon was full when we arrived. Mercedes was placing foil paper strips in the hair of one of her regulars, Beatrice Fernández, a heavyset woman in her forties who had bright pink eyeliner that popped from her brown skin. "You should've let me know you were coming," said Mercedes, walking over to me and wiping her hands on her apron.

"I'm sorry! But look at Benjamin," I said, pointing to my son and his friend, hanging out outside. "He needs a cut, desperately."

Mercedes laughed and shook her head. "You're all going to have to wait," she said, then squinted, examining my hair. "You'll go first. Your hair's a mess, too."

Mercedes grabbed my wrist and directed me to sit in one of the vacant salon chairs. "Denisa," she said, "Can you take care of Luis? Once you're done with Señora Estrada?"

I glanced out the window, and the boys were sitting on the curb, talking. Tony and Noah, who were suburban kids, weren't used to hanging out in this part of the city, especially at a Puerto Rican hair salon.

I leaned back in the salon chair and watched Mercedes, Denisa and Aliyah attend to their customers. You can always tell you're in a Latino salon when you've spent three hours in the chair but haven't had your hair washed yet. All I needed was a glass of coquito to make it authentic.

"So, how's Rebecca?" asked Mercedes after ten minutes, adjusting the paper foils and decorating the head of Señora Fernández.

"Rebecca's great."

"I haven't seen her in over a month," said Mercedes. "I know she's always taking Benjamin to practice."

"It's been too long," I replied. "When are you going to spend the day at our house? You've only been over once."

"Well, Luis, we're always working weekends. It's our busiest time," said Mercedes. "Plus, we don't own a car."

I thought about how we never had a car growing up and had to rely on Chicago's Public Transportation, CTA. Not much had changed for Mercedes. She was still living in the neighborhood, just blocks away from Mom and Dad.

"I can always pick you up. Just…." my voice trailed off as I looked outside. There were pulsing lights and some sort of commotion.

"Oh, Lord! What's this crazy man doing now?" cried Aliyah, staring out the window, blow dryer in hand.

I stood up and noticed Mercedes doing a double take, glancing out the window. "Curse that man," she said, quickly brushing dye into a section of Beatrice's hair, then placing the tinting comb on the counter next to the mirror.

I rushed out of the salon with Mercedes right behind me.

Outside, Benjamin and Noah were standing in front of a cruiser's open passenger door window, arguing with a police officer, whom I couldn't see but assumed was sitting in the driver's seat. The cruiser's red-and-blue strobe lights were blinding, and it took me a half-minute to process what was going on.

"That's an illegal search!" yelled Noah.

"We're not even from here!" added Benjamin.

Mercedes stormed over to the car and pushed aside the two boys, nearly causing them to topple in surprise. "Now, who the hell do you think you are?!" she shouted at the person inside the car.

"Oh, Lord!" said Aliyah, walking up to me. "This is gonna be a rumble!"

"What's going on?" I asked, still in shock.

"They got one of your boy's friends in the back seat," she said, pointing at the car.

"Jesus," I said.

"Oh yes, that's who you need right now," Aliyah agreed.

"You got no right doing this, and you know it! It's barely worth anyone's time," said Mercedes.

I watched as an officer stepped out of the police car. Wearing a black Cordura nylon overshirt carrier and cargo trousers, he was about six feet tall and had a crew cut that obscured the thinning hair at the crown of his head. He looked familiar.

"He had half an ounce of weed on him, ma'am," said the police officer, calmly, as he walked around the front fender of the cruiser and toward Mercedes.

"Don't you dare call me *ma'am!*" warned Mercedes. "I'm no *ma'am* to you. This isn't the South! This is my home. This is Humboldt Park. I'm Señora Morales to you!"

The police officer laughed in a haughty, predatory sort of way. He reminded me of hyenas I had seen on TV.

"I swear to God, you'll regret this if you don't get him out of the car right now," said Mercedes, stepping in his way.

I grabbed Benjamin by the shirt collar and pulled him toward me. His face became flushed, and his eyes turned red. "Weed?" I whispered.

"I don't know, Dad," said Benjamin. "I didn't know he had it, I swear."

I stared at his big brown eyes and saw myself looking back. "Okay. It's okay," I said, squeezing his hand.

"César, I will make life hell for your mother if you take that boy to the station," Mercedes warned.

The police officer's grin disappeared, and I sensed he was getting angry now. *César*, I said to myself. *I can't believe this is César Aguilar.*

"You better watch your mouth," said César, placing his hand on his baton menacingly.

"Like I said, my name is Señora Morales, and I'm just getting started!"

A hush fell over the street corner, and I watched as the two glared at each other, the hyena and the fighting fowl. They stood there for what seemed like ages, steam visibly rising from their nostrils.

At last, I walked toward them. Neither paid me any attention until I was standing just to the side. "César Aguilar? Is it really you?" I asked, breaking the spell.

César turned and looked at me. At first, I could tell he didn't recognize me. I'd gained a little weight since we were teenagers and had a mustache now. César still looked young, but there was a hardness there that only a man could wear.

"César, don't you remember me?" I asked. "Luis Burgos. How long has it been?"

"Luis?" he asked.

"Give me a hug, *bróder*," I said, arms outstretched.

There was an awkward hesitation, and I felt Mercedes' eyes burning holes in the back of my head. César stepped forward and we embraced, patting each other on the back.

"These your kids?" he asked, taking a step back and placing his hand on his holster.

"My son, Benjamin, yes, and his two friends. What's going on?" I asked.

"I need to take this one in," he said, pointing to Tony in the cruiser's backseat. "He had marijuana on him."

"I see."

I turned and looked at Benjamin and Noah. They were staring dejectedly at their feet.

"Well, you gotta do what you gotta do," I said at last. "The Latin Kings are a problem."

Mercedes stepped toward me, but I ignored her. A crowd had gathered outside the salon. Someone in a silver Chevy Cavalier slowly drove by.

César stared at the Chevy for some time. His brow was furrowed and his lips were pursed.

"I'll tell you what," he said. "I'll let him go with a warning"

"Whatever you think is appropriate. You need to follow proper protocols, of course."

"If I catch him with it again, though, it won't be pretty," he said, opening the back door of the cruiser and letting Tony out.

"I appreciate you and your service," I said.

"I thought things would be better here," said César. "But it's like a war zone."

"Yeah, some people think that."

"Just keep an eye on your kids. Gangs are all over the place. I'm not having it. Not on my watch."

"Not everyone's an enemy combatant," said Mercedes.

"Without law and order, we have chaos," said César.

"I just see a lot of people, trying to get by," said Mercedes.

"I'll tell you what...," I said, changing the subject. "You come by my café in Oak Park, El Gallo, and brunch is on me, okay? I'd like to catch up on old times."

César nodded and stepped into the driver's seat of the cruiser. I walked up to the passenger door window and leaned in. "It was good seeing you, César," I said. "Remember the times we would go skateboarding near the fire station?"

César never came by El Gallo. I heard he took a leave of absence from the force eight months after moving to Chicago. The circumstances are still murky, but shortly thereafter, he was gone. Some said he ended up in counseling. Others said that he moved to Mississippi to be closer to his children.

All I know is that he wasn't like the boy I remembered from our childhood. Whatever he had gone through in Iraq was alive and raw and gnawing at him from the inside. The carefree days of our youth had been replaced by a permanent sense of alertness, as if dangers lurked around every corner. That made me sad, because what had really come back from the battlefield was not César Aguilar, but a walking dead man. And because of that, I mourned.

THE EXCHANGE

Near the intersection of West Division Street and North Francisco Avenue were a white Nissan cargo van and a red Chevy Malibu with tinted windows. The two vehicles were idling next to each other on North Francisco Avenue, just out of the way of the passing buses on the cross street, with their passenger-side windows rolled down. The van was facing the park across the street and the sedan was facing the other way, partially blocking traffic in the neighboring lane.

It was midday in early March, and the exhaust from the vehicles was spilling out in wispy plumes in the chilly air. The drivers were engaged in a conversation, and at one point, there was an exchange of some sort.

Luna Burgos was standing at the intersection with her grandfather, Roberto Burgos, waiting for the bus. Luna had recently turned thirteen and had spent Friday and Saturday night with her grandparents at their three-flat down the road. They were bundled in winter jackets, ski caps, gloves and boots. There was a dusting of snow on the ground. Chicago was unconcerned about the predictions of groundhogs.

Luna glanced at the two vehicles, then wrapped her scarf around her face. Roberto, noticing her interest in the cars, placed his arm around her shoulders and redirected her attention toward the park. "There are at least two ways to look at this," he said at last, staring ahead. "I'm going to tell you one way. I'd like to imagine that they are engaged in a type of exchange I was involved in as a youth."

"Go on," said Luna, shivering.

"It was the summer of 1968, and I was sitting on my bicycle near the street curb on Leonard Street in Brooklyn. Next to me, also on a bicycle, but facing the opposite direction, was Bernie Díaz.

"'Take this,' I said, handing him a letter.

"'You know she's seeing Félix Vázquez,' said Bernie nervously. 'He was in the 147-pound weight division for the New York Golden Gloves.'

"'So what?' I said. 'Last time I checked, he didn't win nothing.'

"'He could have, had he not gotten the flu,' said Bernie. 'He's bad news.'

"'I don't think she's really into him,' I said flippantly. 'I can't see her acting all inferior before him, like she needs to know her place as a woman.'

"'Yeah, maybe so. But it's not Josephina I'm worried about.'

"'Look, will you just deliver this letter to your cousin or not!?' I asked, getting annoyed. 'Let me figure out how to deal with Félix.'

"'Okay, okay,' said Bernie. 'I'm just warning you, he's a nut job, and she may not even agree to meet you.'

"'I'm betting she will, Bernie,' I said. 'She just needs a good reason to break free from him.'

"'And you're the reason?'

"'That's right.'

"'Well, maybe he'll win the lottery, end up in South Vietnam, and that'll spare us the trouble,' said Bernie. 'You're lucky you're not eighteen yet.'"

"Were you ever called up for the Vietnam War?" Interupted Luna. "I thought my dad said something happened to you."

Roberto squeezed her shoulders with his right hand.

"All in good time," he said.

"As I was saying, La Casita Spanish and American Food was located off Nassau Avenue across the street from Monsignor Edward J. McGolrick Park. It was a typical Puerto Rican bodega, with Coca-Cola signage under the red awnings and a display of fruits and vegetables in the front window. In the summer, we would place crates of onions, garlic and cabbage out front, next to a gumball machine. It cost a penny to purchase a gumball, and kids were constantly coming by to buy them.

"I worked at the store stocking shelves every day of the week, except for Sundays, for an elderly man named Ezequiel Ramírez. Señor Ramírez, who considered himself a Spaniard even though he was born in Ponce, was the uncle of Aunt Titi, my mother's sister, whom I had been living with over the last six months since immigrating from Puerto Rico. Titi and my uncle, Juan José Cabrera, lived in a crowded, four-story apartment complex close to La Casita. Their two sons, my cousins Manny and Daniel, were grown and no longer lived with them.

"We shared a one-bedroom, rent-controlled apartment not much bigger than a subway car. I slept on a mattress in the living room. I can't imagine how they managed when my cousins were there, but it was a home, anyway, and my ticket out of Fajardo.

157

"I spent most of my time outside the apartment, either working at La Casita or hanging out at McCarren Park with Deigo Colón and Benito Peña, who were my age and lived nearby. Benito, who was darker than me and sported a large afro, also worked for Señor Ramírez and had helped me get the job right after I moved into the neighborhood. We worked different shifts, but that afternoon, seeing it was Saturday and the busiest day of the week, Señor Ramírez had asked us both to help around the shop.

"'I saw her the other day,' said Benito, stocking a shelf with a can of corn.

"'Oh yeah? Where at?' I asked.

"'She was with the Sánchez twins,' said Benito. 'They were walking down Nassau Avenue when we crossed paths. She was dressed all modestly, wearing a skirt down to her knees and a polo shirt. Now, the Sánchez girls...'

"'Did you say anything to them?' I interrupted.

"'Of course, I did. It's not right to walk with your nose to the ground, like no one's there,' said Benito. 'I offered my respects, asking about their families, and so on. I have to give you credit. Josephina is special. She isn't like the rest of the girls around here. She's got a certain quality.'

"I glanced sideways at Benito. I wasn't prone to jealousy, but I wasn't comfortable with him speaking about Josephina in that way in public.

"'I mentioned you had been asking about her,' he said. 'That you wished her well and would like to see her again.'

"'What did she say?'

"'She didn't say anything. She just smiled, then turned to the twins, who were on the verge of laughing. I wouldn't mind getting to know those twins better, I have to say.'

"The door opened, and the hanging brass wall chime rang out. I rose to my feet and looked over the shelves. A woman was pulling her stroller into the store.

"'When are you supposed to meet her?' continued Benito.

"'In an hour,' I said, glancing at the clock above the cash register.

"Benito shook his head. 'Don't take this the wrong way, but you're so fresh, coming from the island. There's a strong preference here for the sophisticated city types.'

"'I wouldn't call Félix *sophisticated*.'

"'Yeah, but his family has been here a while.'

"'My English is better than half the people in Brooklyn. I've been studying it for years. Look,' I said, kneeling to Benito's level, 'I can't wait here any longer. Can you cover for me?'

"'Are you serious?'

"'Yeah, serious, okay? I'll let Ramírez know later,' I said. 'I don't want to explain this to him. If I stay here any longer, I think I'll go crazy,'

"'Shoot, you already crazy!' said Benito. 'Go, then. Just watch yourself, okay?'"

"Was it hard leaving the island, Abuelo?" asked Luna, glancing up at her grandfather.

Roberto nodded, blowing warm breath into his hands.

"I had asked Josephina to meet me at the central pavilion in Monsignor McGolrick Park," Abuelo continued. "It was an oasis among the dilapidated low-rise warehouses, the abandoned lots overgrown with shrubs and littered with trash, the overcrowded, blocky apartment complexes built for function with little consideration for form.

"It was difficult, at first, for me to adjust to this new island. The westernmost edge of Long Island was not what I had envisioned of the mainland while living in Fajardo. I had images of men in suits walking through Wall Street, of women in fur coats attending Rodgers and Hammerstein plays on Broadway. Brooklyn was like Manhattan's bastard half-brother, filled with Puerto Ricans working crap jobs in declining garment factories, struggling to compete with the other undesirables.

"The binary nature of race in the States was confounding and unavoidable. Puerto Ricans, coming in all different colors, were just a type of black, and opportunities to go to decent public schools and to find respectable jobs were bleak. It made no sense to me, with each ethnic group competing for survival at the expense of the other, jockeying for position on the ladder that had room for haves and have-nots, but nothing in between. So much for the so-called melting pot.

"The parks around the city were some of the few equalizers, where anyone could touch nature and disconnect from our troubles. It was invigorating to sit under mature oak trees, and even though I missed the ocean, I knew it had nothing to offer me anymore. The acorns, the saplings sprouting here and there were my new germs of hope. I needed to figure out how to make it here. Or at least, figure out how to get myself on my feet long enough to get the hell out of here. And Josephina was the key to my plan.

"We had spoken a few times, and I swear, I knew she was the one for me the minute I laid eyes on her. She had an inner strength of character unlike anyone I had ever met, and I was convinced that if we were together, we would be fulfilled.

"What I didn't understand was how she got caught up with Félix. Félix represented everything that I hated about Brooklyn. He was a cage fighter who hung out with the wrong crowd. He seemed intent on amplifying all the divisions in the city—picking fights, vandalizing, tearing things down.

"I suppose you could say he was handsome. He was over six feet tall, well-proportioned, square chin. He resembled a browner version of Paul Newman. I honestly think he would have been better off pursuing an acting career. He was theatrical with his emotions. He played the *machismo* schtick to a T.

"And that's where it got him, and me, in trouble. I had been waiting in the pavilion for two hours, bursting with anticipation. 'Will she come?' I asked myself. 'Can't she see Félix is a bad hand?'

"I watched couples ambling past the park benches. I read a flier about the new Puerto Rican Village on Columbia Street. I saw a homeless man stumble past me, holding a brown paper bag. Time seemed to stand still, taunting me. The American flag did not flap on the flagpole. Cars could not be heard blaring their horns.

"And then, out of the corner of my eye, I caught someone walking toward me. The movement was a blur, but it was direct and picking up speed. I heard some laughter. People jeering. I turned, placing my arm against the park bench backrest, and saw Félix sprinting toward me, feet away, now inches, then I was lifted off the bench and thrown to the ground, my right eye burning with pain.

"'You piece of trash,' said Félix, standing over me, waving the letter I had given Bernie for Josephina. 'Who do you think you are, writing this to *my* girl?'

"Félix kicked me in the stomach, causing me to curl up. I saw a group of his friends, six or seven of them, standing behind Félix, cheering him on.

"'Show him his place!' said one.

"'Give him a taste of your boot!' said another.

"He kicked me again, this time in the ribs.

"'Maybe you don't get it, country boy,' said Félix, spitting, 'so let me give you a lesson you won't forget. Don't you ever...' *kick,* 'ever...' *kick,* 'ever mess with another man's woman...' *kick.* 'This is a dog-eat-dog world, *hombre*, and you're my little bitch.' *Kick.*

"His gang of spectators burst out laughing. Félix turned to them, his hands on his hips, grinning broadly.

"I exhaled and, collecting myself, reached for his boots and yanked them toward me. Félix spun his head around in shock, and a moment later, he was on the ground, having landed on his tailbone.

"'Oh, no, he didn't!' said one spectator.

"'He's asking for it now!' said another.

"I tried to bring myself to my feet, keeping my eye on Félix the whole time. It was one thing to fight fairly; it was another thing to jump someone who wasn't even expecting it. I was hurting, but I was not going down this way. I was going to make him work for it, even if I got trounced along the way.

"Félix was furious now. His pride had been injured, I was sure that it was worse than any bruised tailbone. He leapt to his feet and swung his fist at me, barely missing. 'I'm gonna kill you,' he said, and I knew he meant business. 'You shoulda never left the island, *jibarito.*'

"I lifted my fists in front of me, swaying from side to side, as much out of defense as out of dizziness from being hit.

"'You want to fight this way, then? Fine, I'll end you all the same.'

"Félix sprang forward and jabbed me in the ribs, in the same spot where he had kicked me earlier. I grimaced in pain and swung a punch at him, catching only air. He moved forward again and, I have to say, he was the fastest boxer I had ever seen. His jab landed in the same spot, causing me to suck in my breath and stagger backwards.

"He was smiling now. He was a cat playing with his food. He wanted to hurt me, inflict as much pain as possible before dinner. He took another jab, this time hitting my eye, the one that was already beginning to swell shut. A wave of nausea swept over me but shook my head from side to side. 'No, this is not how things are going to end!' I yelled at myself.

"'Finish him, Félix!' shouted someone.

"'He's a rat!' said another.

"I could see that Félix was studying me now, waiting for his last move. He was in a semi-crouching stance, as if ready to spring into a full-blown uppercut.

"And then the spell was broken. There was a high-pitched scream. Panic. Snarling. Tearing of clothes. Puncturing of skin.

"'Holy Jesus!' shouted someone.

"'My leg!" shouted another.

"Félix and I turned and saw an eighty-pound Doberman Pinscher exploding through the gang, knocking them over like bowling pins. The dog tore at their legs, its muzzle covered in blood. They cried, swore and sprinted in every direction out of the park.

"A minute later, the dog was pacing in circles a hundred feet away, sniffing the ground. The sun emerged from a cloud, and I saw Josephina appear as if out of thin air. She walked over to the dog, placed her right hand on its shoulders and glared at Félix.

"'How dare you?' she said, pointing at him. 'How dare you do this to him?'

"'I can do whatever I please,' growled Félix. 'And what are you doing walking up and down the street like this? Having affairs!? You're a whore!'

"I was bleeding and bruised, but this statement hurt me more than anything he had done before. I lunged at him with all my remaining strength, but again, his reflexes were world class. He spun out of my way, elbowing me in the back and causing me to fall face down on the ground.

"'We're *over*,' said Josephina with ice in her veins.

"She snapped her fingers, and the Doberman bared its teeth and leapt at Félix. Félix tried to hit the dog, but a person is no match for a large, athletic Doberman. The dog sank its teeth into Félix's left thigh, causing him to cry out in pain.

"'You bitch!' he screamed.

"'Which one?' asked Josephina, crossing her arms as Félix pulled the dog off and ran.

"The dog followed, nipping at his heels until both were out of sight.

"'She'll come back,' said Josephina, lifting my arm around her slender shoulders. 'I grew up with dogs, and they are one of the few things that keep me safe in this city.'

"'You came,' I said meekly. 'I knew you'd come.'

"'I came, yes, because of that letter,' said Josephina. 'That was a foolish thing to write.'

"'I am a fool for you. I am such a fool for you,' I said.

"Josephina placed her hand gently under my chin, and then, in the briefest of exchanges, pressed her lips against mine.

"'Come with me,' she said. 'We need to get you cleaned up.'

"About nine months later, Josephina and I were married. After our small wedding at the courthouse, and once we were done with school, we packed our bags and left for Chicago. We had to get out of Brooklyn. We heard there were better opportunities out west.

"Félix was called up for Vietnam not long after our altercation and had bigger things on his mind than Josephina and me. I heard that he got involved in the DMZ campaign along with hundreds of other soldiers fighting the Viet Cong. He also got injured in combat, although we don't know for sure. We never heard from him again.

"My encounter with Félix was also fortuitous, in an ironic sort of way. His attack left me with an orbital fracture that took several months to heal and ended disqualifying me for the draft. If I had been sent to Vietnam, who knows if I would be speaking to you right now? Thank God and the blessed Virgin that this was my destiny," said Roberto to his granddaughter.

The bus pulled to the curb on West Division Street, and Luna and Roberto stepped inside. Luna thought about Abuela and the way she always seemed to come to one's defense. She was never aggressive, but if anyone threatened those she loved, watch out!

They took a seat behind the bus driver. The bus was empty, and Luna felt warm by Abuelo's side. Luna glanced out the window and noticed that the vehicles on North Francisco Avenue were no longer there. All that remained were tracks in the snow.

CHANCE THE SNAPPER

You may have heard about the incident with the elusive alligator in the Humboldt Park Lagoon. Some called the alligator Croc Obama. Most, however, gravitated to the name Chance the Snapper, in honor of Chicago-born Chance the Rapper, who was later invited on *The Tonight Show Starring Jimmy Fallon* to discuss the reptile.

This really happened. The five-foot-long alligator, likely someone's abandoned pet, was eventually captured eight days after being reported to Chicago's Animal Care and Control. What the news reports did not state was that Chance the Snapper was not alone. He wasn't even the first of his kind in the lagoon.

Let me explain.

It was late June 2019, about a week after Abuelo's funeral, I was at Abuela's house with my boyfriend, Mikolaj, to check on her at the request of my father. I didn't need my father's encouragement to see Abuela—she had always been a central figure in our lives—but he was worried about her health and believed I had a way of invigorating her.

"When she sees you, she sees herself," he said.

I wasn't sure what to make of that statement. Abuela was decades older than me. I saw little resemblance. Some people said we looked like each other when we were the same age, but I can't say. What I can say is that Abuela was intimidating. She was one of the few people who could beat a person into submission with a look. I once saw her make the insufferable "G" wannabe Henry Castillo *and* his spiky-collared Rottweiler both whimper when she raised an eyebrow.

Mikolaj and I had taken the CTA bus over to Abuela's three-flat on a Tuesday evening and had planned to stay the night to keep her company. Abuela appeared to be in good spirits when we arrived and had prepared *arroz con gandules* and *pasteles*. The *pasteles* were a special treat, and at her age, living alone now, she wasn't up to cooking them from scratch, so she'd picked them up from Lola's across the street.

As we were getting ready to sit at her dining room table, she went to grab the remote to turn off the TV. WGN Channel 9 had been broadcasting a story about the escaped alligator in the Humboldt Park Lagoon all day long. It had become a national story, and the city had hired a gator man from Florida to capture the reptile.

"This is a crazy story, isn't it?" asked Mikolaj.

Abuela said nothing and shook her head from side to side.

"I'm sure this won't be too difficult a job for that alligator trapper," said Mikolaj. "The lagoon isn't that large. You can't possibly lose an alligator there."

"It's cruel to abandon animals like that," I added. "It's all alone, and when the weather drops, it won't survive."

"He's not alone," said Abuela.

"People spend their Sunday afternoons doing picnic brunches by the waters," said Mikolaj. "It's dangerous having him near so many people. Could you imagine him lunging at a kid sitting by the water's edge? Alligators in Disney World have attacked children!"

"What do you mean by him not being alone?" I asked Abuela.

"He's not the only alligator in the pond," she said. "There's another."

"There's another!" exclaimed Mikolaj. "How do you know?"

"I've seen him," said Abuela matter-of-factly. "There's a small alligator and a large one."

"But they've only reported one alligator in the pond," said Mikolaj.

"Go see for yourself," Abuela advised. "The big one. He lives in the marshy area near the waterfall."

"How can it be that you're the only one to have seen him?" asked Mikolaj.

"I assume he doesn't want to draw a lot of attention. He won't bite. He's been there for years."

"For years!" cried Mikolaj.

"The small one caused trouble," said Abuela. "Couldn't keep its head above water. Lurking around, snapping at things. The other one just fits in naturally. Very transparent about its ways. Hard to explain."

"Did the small alligator actually snap at someone?" I asked.

"Yes. It snapped at your aunt Mercedes on the day of the funeral. Caused such a fright! Acting all *macho*. Behaving like that was *his* turf. You know I don't like that sort of thing. That's when I reported him."

"*You* were the one who reported the alligator?" asked Mikolaj, incredulously.

"Just the small one," said Abuela. "We need to clean up the neighborhood."

"How did a large alligator survive winter?" I asked.

"He just burrows into the bottom of the lagoon, I guess. Who knows?"

Mikolaj and I glanced at each other.

"We need to go see for ourselves," I finally stated. "Before it gets dark."

Abuela nodded and pointed to her cabinets. "The gator man will have his hands full," she said. "They've shut down the park, but you can still get in. Just take your dinner with you. Grab some Tupperware from the top drawer, near the refrigerator."

Thirty minutes later, Mikolaj and I were standing under an oak tree near the north side of the lagoon, eating our *pasteles*. The police had cordoned off a section of the park, with an ABC 7 satellite truck parked nearby on Luis Muñoz Marín Drive. We had to keep to the woods, off the trail, to avoid being detected.

For some time, we saw neither alligator nor trapper. It was muggy, and fireflies flickered in the darkening sky and over the lagoon. A bullfrog was bellowing. The lagoon reminded me of the Guaynabo countryside, which we had visited as kids, and I felt at peace. Where else in this part of Chicago could you find such an oasis?

But the peace didn't last long. Close to a graffitied sign that said *POR FAVOR PROTEGER SU LAGO* and PLEASE HELP PROTECT THE LAGOON in large bold letters, were two alligators in a kind of standoff, hissing and rumbling near a patch of purple coneflowers by the shore. One alligator was large, easily ten feet from head to tail, and the other one was about half its size.

The small alligator, later known as Chance the Snapper (Chance for short), appeared to be taunting the larger alligator, which we named Stan from the movie *The Wild*. It was clear that Stan wasn't up for a fight. He was trying to make his way toward the lily pads near the pier, but Chance kept following him, snapping and rumbling, as if he were trying to drive Stan away from the lagoon. At one point, Stan stepped on a muddy spot that someone had tagged with some sort of crude symbol—barrio calligraphy, you might say—causing Chance to lunge at Stan and bite his tail.

Stan hissed in pain, whirling around to confront the smaller aggressor, but despite his size advantage, he was a peaceful creature not accustomed to aggression.

"Better to be a little nobody than an evil somebody," said Mikolaj, his eyes wide in amazement.

"Chance is trying to intimidate Stan!" I cried. "We need to do something."

Stan was walking backwards now, away from the pond, toward the sidewalk that bordered the lagoon. Chance snarled and rumbled, pushing Stan farther from the water, standing tall to make himself appear bigger and badder than he was.

"Where's the trapper?" I asked.

"I don't know," said Mikolaj, picking up a large stone and throwing it into the lagoon.

The splash caught Chance's attention, and he swiveled his head in the sound's direction. Mikolaj picked up another stone and threw it at Chance, missing narrowly, but creating enough of a distraction for Stan to slip by Chance and dive into the lagoon.

Chance was furious and stared at us in that cold-blooded way that meant trouble. Mikolaj threw another stone, this time hitting Chance's back. Chance hissed and swung his tail, then lifted his belly high off the ground and began galloping in our direction, his body undulating as his tail swished from side to side with each stride.

"Oh, snap!" said Mikolaj, realizing the error of his ways.

"Let's get out of here!" I cried.

"I didn't finish my *pasteles*!" replied Mikolaj, shoving a chunk of them into his mouth.

I yanked Mikolaj by his shirt sleeve and was about to run toward the road when we heard an odd gurgling sound, like someone was choking.

"Got ya!" yelled a man from a rowboat by the shore. "You have the right to remain silent!"

Chance hissed and lashed his tail.

"I don't think he's interested in his Miranda rights," said Mikolaj.

"Hush!" I said, letting go of his shirt sleeve.

The trapper had Chance snared around the neck with a hand-held catch pole and was pulling him into his boat. "Saw your eyes shining in the night, you little devil you," said the trapper, his boat now up against the bank.

Chance swung his tail madly from side to side but couldn't break free of the steel wire that tightened further the more he struggled. The trapper tossed a six-foot longboard onto the shore, then leapt from his rowboat, electrical tape in hand, and landed flat on Chance. He pressed his elbow against the gator's snout, then ripped off a piece of tape and, in several swift, looping motions, fastened Chance's mouth shut.

"I'm taking you in, son," said the trapper, lifting Chance onto the longboard and tying him to it with rope. "There's a bounty on you."

Beside a stand of waterlogged cattails, a couple of feet away from the trapper, floated Stan, his head moving from side to side as if to say, "You ain't so tough now, huh, *ese*?"

Later that evening, Mikolaj and I were sitting on the sofa next to Abuela. Mikolaj had his arm around my shoulders, and we were idly watching an episode of *La Piloto* on Univision. It was a good crime drama, one that Abuela and I both liked. I glanced at Abuela and smiled. I suppose, when thinking about it more, we had quite a bit in common. We saw things the same way.

"Are you going to be all right?" I asked her, adding, "I mean, both Mikolaj and I have classes this summer. It's difficult to visit you every week, and you're all alone."

Abuela put her feet up on a small brown ottoman and placed her hand on my knee. "I'm not alone," she said. "There's so much going on in this neighborhood. Never a dull moment."

"That's true," I said, thinking about the lagoon.

"Your *abuelo* may have departed, but he is in good hands now," she said. "And the real *patrón* of this home, he's always been here, watching over us, never abandoning us. We are fortunate. It's not like that alligator filled with bad spirits. The minute I saw him, I knew he had a heavy heart from being dumped by his owners in the lagoon. Unwanted. That's why he lashed out."

"What do you think they're going to do with him?" asked Mikolaj.

"Oh, I don't know," said Abuela. "He'll serve time. There's too much of that nowadays. If he had wanted help out of the *fango*, to wipe the mud off his feet, I would have helped him, but he went around frightening people, causing such a scene. We can't have that in our community. That's not who we are. And if push comes to shove, I'm going to tackle anyone who tries to pull apart the fabric of what holds us together. And that, I'm sure you can see, will keep me plenty busy until the day my *patrón* calls me to his side."

THE HEART IS WHERE WE ROOST

"I've seen you before," I say. "Your moon speckled feathers, your sickle-shaped spur."

I shut my eyes, but he's still there. Large and looming and filled with confidence unlike anything else I've encountered. "You have a way of moving," I say. "You don't just walk about, do you? You strut."

The rooster cocks his head to the side, looking at me with expectant eyes. A short distance away, I see a basswood tree with its heart-shaped leaves.

"But you're not the aggressive type," I say. "You're not charging me, flapping your wings or anything like that. You're just there, like I've always expected you to be."

The rooster pecks at specks of dust.

"Perhaps you're right," I say. "You know, I could give you a heck of a fight. You'd win, of course, but it might delay things, cause a distraction."

The rooster scratches the dirt with its toenails, ignoring my threat. It claws the ground for some time, then rolls on its side, rubbing dust all over its body, flicking it in my direction.

"Enjoying yourself, are you?" I ask.

I watch the rooster massage its hackle feathers, pushing its body along the dusty path in a clockwise direction.

"The wheel of time is ever turning. Earth to earth, ashes to ashes, dust to dust," I say.

The rooster stands up and shakes the excess dust off, so only a thin layer remains. He looks at me again, patiently, but brimming with confidence. He puffs out his breast and widens his feet apart.

"You're not so bad, really. Perhaps misunderstood," I say.

The rooster turns, and I can see its dusky, curving, sickle feathers. It marches along the path, pausing briefly here and there to scratch the ground. I follow from a distance, and soon we arrive at the base of the tree.

I look up at the tree's canopy. It is vast and spreads into the endless night. On one of the lower, furrowed limbs, I see a familiar figure, curled in a ball, tucked against the branch. This makes me smile. And with the slightest breeze to buoy me, I rise with a burst of energy and a flapping of wings, to roost under the hanging cluster of heart-shaped leaves.

ACKNOWLEDGEMENTS

Special thanks to Dr. Kanellos and the Arte Público Press team for giving me a platform for artistic creativity. To Floyd Largent: thank you for your editorial insights and support. And finally, I'm proud and awed at the artistic abilities of my daughter, Jordanna, who contributed to the design of this book cover.